RUNAWAY RIVER

By Verna Elliott Hutlet

This book is a work of fiction. Names, characters, places, and incidents either are products of the author's imagination or are used fictitiously. Any resemblance to actual persons, living or dead, events, or locales is entirely coincidental.

Runaway River

ISBN 978-0-991-7868-5-5

Cover art by Verna Hutlet

Hutlet, Verna Elliott.

Runaway River

1. Fiction 2. Western

First Edition

10 9 8 7 6 5 4 3 2 1

Another adventure for my family and for Gypsy & Condor

1

Madison returned home by Runaway River, so named because the stream broke away from a larger lake at the base of the falls, and escaped down the mountainside as if in a hurry. Madison's parents had requested her not to travel alone any further up into the mountains than Runaway River. It was as if the river separated her from what she knew and what she didn't about the secretive Kaleb family. She had passed this way many times, but this was the first time she happened across Caroline Kaleb fishing where the stream created a quiet cove before continuing down the mountain slope. Madison was nervous to speak to the woman as no one had seen Caroline Kaleb for the past twelve years, other than Caroline's husband. Madison was not sure how the woman would react at having her solitude intruded upon.

Two brown dogs sprawled beside the elderly woman and barely lifted their heads as Madison approached on horseback. Caroline glanced up and shouted to Madison, "Jesse calls them his coon-hounds...to warrant his Papa feeding them, but they haven't treed a raccoon in their lifetime." Madison laughed and was instantly drawn to the woman's humor.

Caroline wore a wide-brimmed straw hat, her tresses sprayed out from beneath the brim like silver moonbeams. A lacy, pink ribbon circled the crown of her hat and added femininity to an otherwise masculine pair of men's overalls and over-sized work boots. Caroline patted the grass beside her, beckoning Madison to come join her at the stream's edge.

"Only caught one fish so far this afternoon," Caroline complained. "Jesse says it's 'cause I won't put live worms on my hook...Always felt sorry for the little suckers."

Madison's forehead wrinkled into a quick wince at Caroline's acknowledgement of Jesse in the present tense, but she grinned at the woman's refusal to use worms as bait. Madison knew Jesse to be dead, but she did not contradict Caroline's chatter. In fact, after a short time, it was easy to sit beside Caroline Kaleb on the edge of Runaway River and enjoy the woman's amusing tales about her son. Caroline's fantasy made Jesse seem almost real, and gave hope to Madison that there was a hero; a perfect prince somewhere out there, even if he was just in Caroline's imagination.

"Oh, he's not without his faults," Caroline confessed, after a lengthy conversation on the praises of her son's virtues. "He's an angel and never forgets to care for everything and everybody...but he forgets my goats. I swear he does it deliberately to tease me. I have to feed them myself to make sure their chores are done." The sparkle of motherly love in Caroline's eyes made it easy for Madison to leave the woman in her dream world.

Madison's father had spoken of Jesse's death many times, explaining how Jesse's horse had wandered away from an open corral in the early spring when mountain rivers were swollen from the first melt. Jesse had gone in search of his yearling, and was crossing the river on rocks that jutted above the river current to make a footbridge, when a flash flood thundered down Runaway River, and washed the young boy away. Andy couldn't look at the horse after that, so he gave the animal to her father. The story had always interested Madison because she inherited Timber, Jesse's mountain horse.

For weeks, the whole valley searched the riverbanks for Jesse's body, but it wasn't until months later that someone found a youth's body far downstream, and figured it must be Jesse, as no other child had been reported missing. Folks put their money together and had a nice pine box made for the boy before notifying Andy. They figured there was no sense in Andy and Caroline seeing their child in that condition.

Andy Kaleb had nodded a silent, solemn thank you, slid the pine box into the back of his wagon and returned to the mountains. No one knew where they buried the boy. No one saw Caroline again, and Andy only came down out of the mountains occasionally to sell produce and buy supplies. Andy never spoke to anyone about Jesse again. When he came to the Graham farm every fall to purchase extra winter-feed for his stock, he would merely ask her father about Jesse's horse. Perhaps conversing about the colt was Andy Kaleb's way of acknowledging that his son once lived.

Madison rose to remount her horse and say goodbye to Caroline.

The woman remained seated by the river, holding her fishing rod in both hands. She turned to look up at Madison's horse; a handsome dark bay with an evergreen shaped star on his forehead. "Is that Timber?" she questioned, and Madison nodded shyly, somewhat surprised that Caroline could deal with the reality of Jesse's horse belonging to someone else, and yet not acknowledge her son's death.

"Always was a handsome colt," Caroline stated. "Has some Spanish blood in him...did you know that? Wild horse ancestry from the conquistadors."

"I didn't know that," Madison smiled. "He's very sure-footed in the mountains and sensible head. Never spooks."

Caroline smiled back. "I know...Jesse told me." Then she faced the river again and threw out her line."

Madison decided to say nothing to her family about her encounter with Caroline Kaleb at the fishing hole. To gossip about Caroline's fantasy would be like betraying Caroline, and there was something exciting about keeping a secret, as long as it didn't hurt anybody.

ঙ্গ

Andy arrived at the Graham farm in late autumn, as was his custom, to buy bags of grain from Madison's father before winter hit the mountain plains. Madison kept her distance, and did not speak to the man, not wanting to put him in a position of embarrassment if he knew she knew about his wife's fantasies. After Andy drove his wagon back up the mountain trail, Madison sat down on the bench outside the woodshed and sighed.

Troy Bennett had cheated on her. That is all she could concentrate on this morning. Being demoted to second place in someone's heart was hard to bear. She saddled Timber and informed her family she was visiting her friend, Bess for the day. They looked at her with sympathetic eyes and nodded with understanding.

Bess was busy watching four younger siblings and had little time to listen to Madison's concerns over Troy Bennett. Madison concluded it was never a good time to confide about personal matters if you are interrupted every time you're about to pour your heart out, so she kept her visit short with preoccupied Bess. Not wanting to return home so early, Madison aimed for the solitude of Runaway River where she could sit by the stream and contemplate on what to do about Troy Bennett.

Madison had recently learned about Troy's secret visits to another girl in a neighboring village. She longed to be numbed against the truth of it and suddenly, Caroline's fantasies seemed a haven to escape to. Andy's fresh wagon trail stretched upward into the mountains like two beckoning arms. Throwing caution away, Madison accepted the lure of it, and for the first time in her life, travelled higher into the mountains than Runaway River.

Now, after having travelled far up into the mountains to visit Caroline on their mountain farmstead, Madison did not know how to tell her parents about her impulsive journey. She pulled her horse to a stop and dismounted. The wind was picking up and daylight was fading fast behind a storm cloud approaching over the mountain range. She could see clusters of bluebells and brown-eyed susans scattered amongst the waving grasses in a clearing, and hurried to grab a few fistfuls to make a bouquet for her mother.

Madison held the bluebells in her hands and sighed. She didn't like concealing the full truth about where she had gone today. A partial truth was like wearing one boot and trying to walk as if nothing was out of the ordinary.

A swirl of autumn leaves followed Andy Kaleb into the old cabin before he could slam the door shut against the storm. "Going to be a two-dayer," he called to his wife, kicking off his boots and walking across the wooden floor to dump an armful of firewood into a worn wood box beside the fireplace. He returned to hang his hat and wet slicker on a peg close to the door entrance. A second hat rested over an adjacent peg, and with an affectionate pat, Andy Kaleb reached over and brushed dust off its wide brim.

Caroline tucked a fall of grey hair behind one ear, and continued to set the table for three. "Then I hope Jesse has remembered to close the door to the goat shed. He gets so mindful of the dogs that he forgets all about my goats."

"He'll remember," Andy soothed, putting a loving arm about her shoulders and giving her a reassuring hug.

They sat down at the table and she reached over to pour a cup of coffee for her husband. "Madison was here today. Did you see the flowers she brought me?" She pointed to a bouquet of wild flowers, vibrant against the aged pine cupboards and cabin walls.

Andy's mouth dropped open in surprise and concern. "She came here...all by herself?"

"Don't worry. She promised to keep to your fresh trail from this morning."

"Yes, but," Andy stuttered, not able to reveal his true concern about Madison's visit, "...but there's wildlife in these mountains, and harm could come to her."

"She can shoot a pea out of a pod at fifty feet," Caroline huffed, shrugging her shoulders to dismiss his fears, "...and she rides that old mountain horse that Jesse gave her, and you know that horse is as sure-footed as a mountain goat and would never spook on her."

"True...but storms come up fast in the mountains and you can get caught before you know it." Lines formed between Andy's eyes and his forehead wrinkled with anger. "I don't know what's wrong with Mel's head, allowing his daughter to roam these mountains all by herself like that. That puma will get her one of these times."

Caroline looked up at the kitchen window, as the wind and rain rattled loose panes against the frame. A lonesome whistle escaped through the cracks like a howling coyote. "She'll be safe back down in the valley by now. It was nice to share tea with her."

Andy knew it was no use to argue. "The flowers are nice," he sighed, and threaded a row of peas on his fork as he deliberated on how to discourage Madison Graham from visiting Caroline again.

Caroline's mental state was fragile after their son's death. The only thing that kept Caroline functional was a mental block against the truth of Jesse's death. For the past twelve years, she had lived in a fantasy world, continuing on with her daily life as if Jesse was alive, still setting a plate at the table for him, still washing one of his shirts and hanging it beside their own on the clothes line.

At first, Andy understood her denial was a way of handling the loss of their son, and he figured after a time, she would face the sad truth of Jesse's death. But months passed and then years, and now he had to admit, he had grown accustomed to seeing Jesse's plate set at the table and his son's hat hung beside his own near the doorway. Jesse was all they had. They were not hurting anyone with their fantasy, but Madison might interfere if she thought

Caroline's mind wasn't right. He had to think of a way to stop the young lady from returning.

The Kalebs lived high on a mountain range where the land leveled flat enough to allow for a small homestead between the towering pines and rocky cliffs. A faint wagon trail was the only connection between the Kalebs and the village of Northfork below. Andy travelled down into the valley occasionally to sell firewood, a few furs and a goat or two, which brought enough return for kerosene for their coal-oil lamps and wax for making candles, flour and sugar, a bolt of cloth and thread for Caroline, and a supply of nails, tools, matches, and other essentials for himself. Late in the fall, Andy travelled only as far as the Graham farm and traded produce for a winter's supply of grain for his stock, but other than that, he and Caroline lived in recluse. They produced enough hay for their few livestock, and vegetables, meat, and eggs for themselves, and needed little else from the valley.

As for companionship, Andy had once worried that Caroline might need the friendship of others, but she had shown no sign of loneliness throughout the years, instead happily sharing her friendship with the farm animals and dogs and an occasional pet from the wild. He knew some would question such solitude and consider it unhealthy, but he feared the alternative might only bring endless depression to Caroline. Reality would have to be Jesse dying all over again.

"Did the girl say why she came?" he quizzed, not fully understanding why a young lady would spend hours riding up into the mountains to see folk who were not even of any relation. This had to be the last time she visited.

"She didn't say...but," Caroline half whispered, and covered her mouth to suppress a little giggle,"...I think she comes because she likes Jesse."

Andy's eyes grew wide with fear. "Sh...She knows about...Jesse?"

"Well, of course. He gave her that horse when he was eleven. Remember? After the river burst, the horse escaped to Graham's, and Jesse said Megan could keep the colt."

Andy looked across at Jesse's empty plate. Her story was partially true, except it was Andy who had given Mel Graham the horse after Jesse's death, not Jesse.

"What...did you discuss about Jesse?" He prayed Madison would not return home with stories about Caroline's mental state. He feared good intending people from the outside might force Caroline to face the truth of Jesse's death, and that would destroy her world.

"Madison never says much...just smiles," Caroline said softly. "I told her Jesse had grown into a fine handsome fellow, and she said she was going to marry him someday. Isn't that sweet?" Caroline laughed out loud and Andy was so delighted to hear his wife laugh, he set aside his worry about Madison endangering Caroline's world of fantasy. He doubted Madison would visit again.

With supper over, Andy picked up his violin, sat in the homemade, pine rocking chair, and played a zesty polka to drown out the howling wind. Caroline retrieved dishes from the table and then suddenly, in a spurt of youthful spirit, she gave a little twirl to the music that made her apron billow out from her cotton dress. Andy laughed and coaxed her to dance even more. With dish plates held high above her head, Caroline spun again and again until Andy had to put a leg out to stop her from twirling right into the hearth of the fireplace. Yes, she was happy in her fantasy world, and Madison Graham was not going to ruin that.

2

Madison had barely removed her riding boots in the entranceway, when her brother stuck his head around the kitchen door and shouted, "Troy was here three times today, looking for you. What on earth could you and Bess possibly talk about for eight hours?"

"You and all your faults," she kidded back, and threw a rolled-up sock at his head. Madison's face sombered when her mother appeared beside her brother in the kitchen doorway. Loretta Graham dusted flour off her hands and peered at Madison over the brim of her glasses. Madison knew that suspicious look, and lowered guilty eyes to the floor.

She quickly confessed to her mother and brother, "I didn't stay all day with Bess. She was busy, so I rode up into the mountains for awhile...I needed to think a bit...about Troy and me." She handed the cluster of wild flowers to her mother, but now the flowers seemed more like a bribe for mercy than a gift.

"Aaah, give the guy another chance," Timothy sympathized with her former boyfriend. "He looked pretty sorry this afternoon."

Madison thought her brother would make a good minister as forgiveness came easy to him, but she was not able to forgive Troy Bennett so quickly. "Was he sorry he cheated...or sorry he got caught?" she flung back.

Timothy scrunched his face up as if he had been punched in the stomach. "Oooo! Troy's going to pay for this mistake." Then he laughed and disappeared out of the room, not wanting to get any deeper involved in his older sister's relationship with the neighbor's son.

"I'll put these pretty flowers in water, and heat up your supper," Loretta said with a sympathetic voice, and returned to the kitchen behind Timothy.

"Maybe later. Okay, Mom!" Madison said with a tired, strained voice. "I feel like lying down for a bit." Her journey to and from the Kaleb homestead had taken six hours and she was exhausted. She raced upstairs to her room before her mother could reply. She knew her family believed she was distraught over Troy and probably needed some alone time, but strangely, that was not the case anymore. Since meeting Caroline, her whole world had changed. She had become enthralled with Caroline's tales about the ghost of Jesse Kaleb. Troy couldn't hold a candle to Jesse, except for the fact that Troy was alive and Jesse wasn't.

Madison flung herself across her bed and stared at the adjacent wall where the setting sun cast shadows through lacy curtains. The light and shadows created a magical, dancing effect on the wall and she let it hypnotize her. Soon rain clouds would drop down out of the mountains and take away the reflections on the wall, but for now, she could lay in another world with her heart pounding in her chest, and excitement racing across the surface of her skin.

She questioned her own feelings. What was wrong with her? She knew Jesse was dead, so why did she enjoy the afternoon so much with Caroline, laughing about things she said Jesse had done, yet knowing it was all in Caroline's imagination. Why did she enjoy helping Caroline bake cookies for an imaginary son who would never eat them? Madison smiled to think of the time Caroline said Jesse had chased a squirrel out of the house with a broom, tripped over the slop pail for the pigs, and landed flat on his back covered in potato water, apple peels and carrot tops. She could see the comical incident so vividly in her mind that it seemed impossible not to have happened. She put her hand over her mouth to stifle a laugh.

She knew when she left the Kaleb farmyard that the barn was in need of repair, corrals were broken down, and the potato patch was weedy from lack of tillage. If Jesse existed, he would have repaired such things and helped in the fields. Madison wasn't blind, but at the same time, Caroline had managed to draw her into a fanciful world, and it was a peaceful escape from the hurt of Troy's deception. Madison didn't want to step back into harsh reality. Maybe Caroline didn't want to either.

❧

"Going to have to fix those loose window panes before winter's on us," Andy commented, "or they'll be gathering frost as thick as a fence post." He put on his slicker to take one last check on the livestock before going to bed, and grabbed a rifle from the corner of the room.

"Check on the dogs in the barn too," Caroline suggested, as she placed a lantern in his free hand. "I thought I heard them bark a few times when you were playing the fiddle. Could be that puma sniffing out the goats in the shed. Be careful."

Andy stepped out into the cold rain, which made him shiver beneath the thin slicker. Winter wasn't far off. He hurried across the yard, and rounded the corner to make sure the goat-shed door was closed against the storm and wildlife. He saw movement by the corral and slowly placed the lantern handle over the top of a corral post, so he could use both hands on the rifle. Slow and deliberate, he raised his rifle to his shoulder, and peered into the shadows to focus on what appeared to be movement beside the corral. It was raining hard now, so he highly doubted the puma would be anywhere except in his nice dry mountain cave somewhere high in the mountains. Suddenly, a horse stepped out of the shadows and into the lantern's path of light. With relief, Andy lowered his rifle. He half expected it to be that old black bear around again, hoping the pigs had left some apples and scraps in the troughs. No rider appeared to be in the saddle and the reins dangled aimlessly to the ground. After a moment, Andy rethought caution and raised his rifle once more to circle his gaze about the farmyard.

"Anyone here? Hello!," he shouted, and the red chestnut trotted off a few paces at the sound of a stranger's voice. It was then that Andy noticed the limp body being dragged by one foot caught in a stirrup. "Whoa," Andy soothed the horse, and quietly opened the corral gate. He carefully herded the horse into the corral and shut the gate behind him. Now he could approach the horse without frightening the animal back into the darkness of the forest. The chestnut horse moved away slightly as Andy approached, so Andy moved slowly, speaking in a low quiet voice until the horse stood still. Andy quickly unbuckled the girth of the saddle and let the saddle slip to the ground. He could then easily remove the man's foot from the stirrup without the horse taking off with its victim.

In the rain, the lantern only cast a faint glow across the corral, and all Andy could do was hope the rider was still alive. He tried to find a pulse but the man's body and his own fingers were both so ice cold, he wasted no more time trying to find a heart beat. He hated to frighten Caroline, but it was necessary to bring the man into the house, dead or alive. He struggled in the rain, but finally managed to hoist the body over his shoulder, hook the lantern over his arm, grab the rifle and hit for the house. There was no time to worry about the saddle lying in the muddy corral. If the rider was still alive, he might be clinging to his last breath, so Andy hurried to get him out of the punishing weather.

Andy kicked at the kitchen door several times with the toe of his boot, seeing as both hands were full with the body, lantern and rifle. Caroline opened the door in bewilderment at his strange knocking, and her mouth gasped as Andy carried in the body and lowered him onto a cot nestled in a corner of the cabin.

"My God," Caroline cried in anguish to the unconscious young man, as she grabbed his cold hand and began rubbing it vigorously to encourage blood circulation. "What have you gone and done to yourself, Jesse?"

"Found him with his foot caught in the stirrup out by the corral. Lucky I went to check on the goat shed or he'd be frozen solid by midnight." Andy bent over close to the body, seeking a sign of breath coming from his nose and mouth. "Yep! Yep! He's still breathing, but we best get him out of these wet clothes and start warming him up. Warm some towels and blankets by the fire, Caroline. I'll get some of my dry clothes on him."

With dry clothes and warm blankets bundled about the young man, and an old, iron foot-warmer tucked in near his feet, the Kalebs sat in guarded watch, waiting and hoping for an encouraging sign that the stranger was gaining consciousness.

"I think he might have bumped his head when he fell off the horse," Andy thought out loud. "Has a bruise on his forehead. Might need a doctor."

Caroline said nothing, and just sat with her hands in her lap, twisting her apron nervously until it resembled a rope. She stared into the young man's pale face and bit her lip anxiously. Suddenly, she blurted, "I've told him a hundred times to keep his eye on the weather in these mountains. But young folk have a mind of their own. He should have been home from the wood lot hours ago. Likely trying to fall an extra tree or two before coming home."

Andy patted her on the shoulder, and rose to throw some more logs on the fire.

The young man moaned and attempted to roll onto his side. A flurry of arms rushed to his side, and tried to coax his eyes open. Finally, his eyes fluttered open and he looked about the room in bewilderment. Then he focused in on two strange faces whose noses almost touched his own.

"What's your name, son?" Andy questioned, and the young man looked at him blankly. He opened his mouth to reply, frowned and then shook his head.

"He's just testing your memory," Caroline chipped in cheerfully, relieved to see him awake. "Looks like you bumped your head when you fell off your horse. Now you just rest, Jesse, and I'm going to get you some nice warm soup."

As Caroline bustled about the cook stove, Andy once more questioned the stranger. He kept his voice lowered so Caroline couldn't hear. "Do you know where you came from?"

The young man closed his eyes, as if searching for the answer inside his head. Then he reopened his eyes and shook his head.

Andy tried once more to extract some knowledge from the young man before Caroline completely embedded a false identity into his head. "Do you recall what happened?"

The stranger thought for a moment. "I remember the rain cutting into my eyes like ice...Then my horse slipped...and I felt us both going down...and that's all I remember."

"What were you doing way up in the mountains at this time of year?" Andy asked, knowing few passed this way even in summer time.

The stranger shook his head, for he remembered nothing beyond the moments before the fall.

"Well, here comes the wife with some soup. You eat up and warm your belly. You'll likely remember more in the morning."

Several weeks passed, and the winds in the mountains took on a crispness that made the men tuck their chins deep into their collars as they walked towards the barn. The chill of night had transformed raindrops into snowflakes earlier in the day, but now the sun had melted away their whiteness, except in shady patches along the timberline. Anyone who knew the mountains realized that these were the forerunner signs of winter.

The young stranger had recuperated from his mishap, except for his memory. Small bits and pieces of memory did not reveal who he was or where he came from. As far as Caroline was concerned, the young man was Jesse. He somewhat shyly accepted her motherly love and affection with a mixture of gratitude and slight confusion.

The young man was now well enough to join Andy with barn chores. "There's no sense you taking off with no memory," Andy advised him, pulling his coat collar up to block the cold north wind. "Winter's rolling in and I got no time to take you around to places to check on where you come from. Feel bad about it, cause there's likely a ma and pa out there somewhere, or a wife worried to death about you...but I gotta buck up more wood for the winter or we'll be burning the furniture to keep warm...and I can't leave Caroline alone with winter nipping at our heels."

Three sows waddled out of a shed as Andy tossed a pail of barley and food scraps into their pig trough. The young man nodded in understanding, and forked a bundle of hay to his horse in the corral. "Sorry I've caused you this trouble, sir."

"You're no trouble, son. Kinda nice company." Andy slapped him affectionately on the shoulder. "I'm just running late this fall, that's all. Should have had the bucking done so the firewood was reading for splitting, but these old legs are moving slower every year. You're welcome to stay for the winter. Maybe help a bit here and there to pay for feed for your gelding. Come spring, your memory will likely be back. If not, I'll take you down into the valley and over to Riverflat territory, and we'll try to find out who you are. Best I can do."

The young man nodded in grateful acceptance. Then he hesitated and awkwardly asked, "Your wife calls me Jesse. Does she...think I'm someone?"

Andy gave a carefree little laugh. "Aah, never you mind. She adopts every stray who passes by; cat, dog, raccoon. To her, you're all her children. Besides, you gotta have a name and I guess Jesse is as good as any. Right?"

"Fine by me," the young man shrugged and laughed back. "Jesse it is." As they mounted the veranda steps, Jesse turned and looked across the yard at a large pile of fallen trees. "You fall all that by yourself?"

"Yep!," Andy said proudly. "Took me near all summer falling, and near all fall dragging them home out of the bush one by one with the old roan. Skat's a riding horse, not bred for hauling heavy logs out of the forest, but he does a good job, so long as I lighten the load to one log at a time for him. Slow going though."

"Best we get bucking the logs up tomorrow," Jesse suggested, looking up at the sky as a feather dusting of snow wet his eyelashes. "You have a good sharp saw to cut the logs up with?"

"The sharpest."

"An axe to split them with?"

"The sharpest."

"Then we're in business," Jesse smiled, and they entered the cabin to the aroma of chicken and dumplings and fresh apple pie.

3

Madison sat on the top railing of the corral and looked off towards the mountains. She wouldn't be able to return to the Kaleb homestead until spring now, as snow would soon bury the trail deeply, and only a dog sled team, or someone on snowshoes would chance reaching the Kalebs until spring thaw. She looked down sadly at the ground between her knees. She felt lost, caught between wishful fantasy and reality.

Troy had visited many times in the last few weeks and tried to explain away his involvement with another lady in the neighboring village. Madison wished instead of making excuses that he had come right out and said he liked the other girl and that was that. There was no use him telling her that he was tricked into a double date by his friend, Chad Tazino, and then continued to see the other girl a few times so he wouldn't offend her. Madison highly doubted Troy would think in such a chivalrous manner. He was the kind that never remembered a birthday except his own. No matter what Troy's excuses, she found it hard to trust him again...and the worst part was, she felt like she had betrayed him as well, because she had been captivated by the stories of Jesse.

It was difficult trying to end a relationship with Troy. He was the neighbor's son and her brother's best friend, even though Troy was several years older than her brother. She had grown up with Troy, almost like a sister to him, playing with kittens in their loft, walking to school with him every day, fishing and going to community dances together. Everyone around Northfork matched them up as a pair even as children, and it was very difficult to destroy a community plan.

A voice jolted her from behind. "A penny for your thoughts." Her seventeen-year-old brother mounted the fence and straddled the railing, facing her. Timothy was a lanky teenager, three years younger than herself. "What's up, sis?" He tilted his head to one side, peering into her face. When she didn't answer, he inquired further. "There's more to this Troy thing than you're saying, isn't there? Something else is bothering you."

Madison looked at him timidly, not sure if she should mention Jesse's name to anyone. "Did you ever...I mean...can you remember...Jesse Kaleb?"

"No! I was pretty young when he used to come with his father to get feed in the fall. He never went to school here either, so few in the community ever saw him. Why?"

"Do you think there's a possibility that the body they found wasn't his?" She focused on the mountains again, unable to look her brother straight in the eye, for she had not told any of her family about the two meetings she experienced with Caroline.

Timothy frowned and followed the drift of her eyes to the mountains. "Why would you ask something like that? It's gotta be over ten...twelve years since their boy was killed in the flash flood. Of course, it was Jesse's body. No one else was missing."

"Yes, I know it looks that way...but...could there be a chance it wasn't? Did anyone ever identify the body?"

"The doc, I suppose. Folks had him in a coffin when Andy picked him up, so guess doc was the only one. Where are you going with this?"

Madison thought for a few moments, not knowing if she should reveal her secret meetings with Caroline to her brother or not, but she was thirsty for more knowledge about Jesse.

"I met Caroline...Mrs.Kaleb...in the mountains... twice," Madison finally confessed, "once at the fishing hole by Runaway River...and once at their homestead. She pretends...or thinks Jesse is still alive. A mother can sense these things. I kind of half believe her." Madison was now desperate for someone to agree with the possibility that Jesse could still be alive, but she could tell by the shocked look on Timothy's face that it was not going to be her brother. She instantly regretted having mentioned Jesse to him.

"Sakes alive!" Timothy exclaimed in horror, "And you believe her? She's lived up in those mountains with nary a person to talk to except Andy for over a decade. She's likely as spinny as a wagon wheel, imagining all sorts of people coming and going around her."

"Actually, I found her very nice." Madison spoke up in Caroline's defense. "And I can't wait until spring to visit her again, and find out more about Jesse."

Timothy's mouth set in a firm straight line, and he jumped down from the corral. "You stay out of those mountains or that old puma will get you. Troy cheated and hurt you, sis. I'm sorry about that...but you have to get a grip on yourself. You're starting to act as spinny as that old lady in the mountains." He turned and walked towards the house, kicking several stones out of the way with an angry swipe of his foot. Things were so less complicated when Troy and Madison were dating.

Madison jumped down from the corral and followed him in haste. She yelled at his back, "Don't you go telling my business to Mom and Father."

Timothy whirled around and there was anger in his voice. "It's too late to shut the gate after the bull is out, Maddy. You've told me things about Andy's wife and for your safety, I'm telling the folks. Maybe they can fill you in on a few things. Get your head screwed back on straight before you get into trouble." He turned back towards the house, his stride long in comparison to hers. She ran to keep up to him.

"C'mon, Tim. I told you those things in confidence."

"No, you told me those things because you had a guilty conscience and you wanted to dump on someone. If you want to unload stuff like that on me, then you have to give me the respect to know what to do with the information."

"All I asked about was if there was a possibility Jesse could be alive."

"And you travelled all by yourself far up into the mountains and visited Caroline Kaleb without telling a soul where you were, without thinking of the danger that could possibly have happened to you, and without any thought to dozens of people who might have risked their lives to search the mountains looking for you. What's gotten into you?"

Madison stomped off angrily to the house ahead of him. She realized Timothy had good reason to tell her parents about her secret meetings with Caroline, and she knew her family would give her a sound scolding and issue reasoning of why Caroline clung to the belief that her son was alive, but Madison didn't want to listen to reasoning. She wanted to believe in Caroline's fantasy. She wanted Jesse to be alive.

ଓଃ

Troy Bennett stared at Timothy with his mouth partly open. Then he laughed and relaxed his shoulders. "You're just kidding me."

"No, I'm not," Timothy assured him. "Caroline Kaleb has got Madison believing Jesse is still alive, and she's determined to pursue the possibility. She says his body wasn't truly identified, so nobody knows for sure."

"Why would Madison care? The Kaleb kid's been gone for at least a dozen years." Troy threw his arms up in the air in bewilderment. "Madison doesn't even know these people."

"Well, she's beginning to know them. She's secretly visited with Caroline twice in the mountains. Don't ask me why." Timothy sighed. "Father scolded her good last night for taking off into the mountains alone without telling anyone where she was going, and for listening to Caroline's ramblings, but when Maddy gets something in her head, she's like granite to break. She's completely spell-bound by stories of him."

"That's ridiculous," Troy snarled angrily, a tinge of jealousy suddenly warming his temperament. "What's so special about a mountain kid who has never seen mankind for years and can likely only talk in grunts. He better not even look sideways at her or he'll wish he never popped up from the grave."

Timothy nodded in agreement. "Yeah, she has to know he's dead."

Troy shook his head in despair. "How many times does a man have to say I'm sorry? I messed up. I've admitted that a dozen times to her. Well, I hope she keeps this fantasy within your family and doesn't start talking to others about it. Banker Owens just gave her that job at the bank, starting in April when Bob Henderson retires. He'll not be hiring a fool, so she better smarten up."

Timothy glanced off towards the mountain range. "Do you think we should check on the Kalebs...and this ghost of a Jesse...for Maddy's sake? It might be good to put these stupid ideas of hers to rest before she starts spouting off her thoughts to Bess...'cause if she tells Bess, the whole valley's going to hear about it."

"Well, that's for sure," Troy agreed, as he shifted from one foot to the other. Troy was a few years older than Timothy, and knew the mountains and the danger of unexpected weather, especially this close to winter. Folk had perished trying to cross the high range late in the season. He pondered for a few minutes and shook his head. "We'll leave it be until spring. Madison won't be going there again until spring anyway, and hopefully by then, she'll have come to her senses and this foolishness will be over."

Andy and the young stranger stood on opposite sides of the log, each holding tight to the handles on the saw. They began sawing back and forth in a continuous rhythm, watching the sawdust fall upon their boots. As the day progressed, the pile of wood blocks grew taller. By nightfall, they were pleased with their efforts, and stretched their tired arms and backs on their way to the house.

"Should have it all blocked in a week at this rate," Andy cheerfully stated, as they entered the house. "It would have taken me half the winter without you. Good job."

Jesse nodded and smiled back, glad to repay their kindness in some small way. He poured hot water from the kettle into a basin of cold water, and held his blistered hands longer than normal under the warm water, but never issued a word of complaint.

At the dinner table, Andy caught sight of Jesse's blistered palms, and reached out to turn one hand over. "Should have given you thicker gloves."

Jesse stared at his raw hands. For a fleeting moment, he visioned a revolver lying in his hand, and suddenly winced. Then the image was gone.

"Remember something?" Andy quizzed, and Jesse shook his head. He didn't think the flashback was something wise to mention at this time.

"You know, I think we'll skip a day of bucking tomorrow, and fix that stall and feed bunker in the barn. First blizzard and your gelding will need to come in the barn. Should arrange a stall and manger for him beside Scat. You good with a hammer?"

"Guess we'll find out," Jesse answered with a smile. He figured Andy had changed jobs to give his hands a day to heal, and he warmed to the kindness of the older man.

Caroline sat across the table, drinking in Jesse's grey-green eyes and sandy curly hair, which curled along his neckline from lack of a barber. She pushed a plate of cinnamon buns towards him. "They used to be your favorite."

Jesse glanced quickly at Andy, and then back to Caroline. "And always will be," he said with a quiet smile, reaching out and plucking the biggest bun from the top, which he knew she had deliberately placed there for him. Jesse had come to realize on his own that Caroline viewed him as her son. He did not question Andy further about it, feeling Andy would tell him more when he wanted to. For now, he could hear the cold wind outside and was grateful to share the warmth of their home and hospitality, and to be thought of as a son.

Jesse lay on his cot in the corner of the kitchen and let his sore muscles sink into the straw-padded mattress. The Kalebs had gone to bed, and he was alone with his thoughts. He held his one hand out and stared at it, trying to bring back the image of the gun that had previously flashed across his mind. The kind of gun that a man wore could tell a lot about a man. He looked at his thumb and with relief, saw no callus there, which meant he was not one accustomed to much shooting.

Jesse slipped quietly out of bed and crossed the floor to Andy's gun belt hung by the doorway. The revolvers appeared dusty, as if it had been some time before they were used for any purpose. He pulled a revolver out of the holster and held it in his hand, trying to rebirth the image that had appeared to him earlier. The gun felt heavy and awkward in his hand. He had seen experienced gunmen twirl their pistols and gave it a try. The gun flipped out of his hand and he caught it quickly before it fell to the floor and awakened the Kalebs.

Words came to him in the darkness of the room; harsh deep words that intimidated him. "If you're any kind of a man, you'll avenge his death some day." He could vision the gun being forced into his hand by a much stronger hand. "Don't come back until you're man enough to use it." He tried to remember more, but nothing further surfaced in his mind. He sighed and returned the gun to its holster. He could remember the gun and the words of the man who put it in his hand, but he couldn't remember who he was supposed to avenge or why. He didn't think the memory would endear him to the Kalebs, so kept silent about it.

The next morning, Jesse asked Andy if he could take the revolvers out and practice shooting with them. Andy was somewhat surprised but agreed, thinking it probably normal for a young man to want to target practice once in awhile.

For Jesse, he simply wanted to see how good he was with a gun. It didn't take him long to realize he couldn't hit a bottle if it was sitting an arm's length away. He turned to Andy, who was leaning against the shed with a somewhat dismayed look on his face.

"I guess I'm not a gunfighter," Jesse grinned, and Andy nodded his head in full agreement.

"Be thankful for small blessings," Andy said to Jesse. "But should you want to improve, I suggest you first learn how to hold the gun steady and aim." He walked over to the young man and took the revolver. Andy held his arm out straight like a rifle barrel and let his eyesight follow down his rigid arm. Pow went the gun! Jesse flinched at the sound, but Andy did not. A twig flew off a tree far in front of them.

Jesse asked with humor, "Was that a hit or a miss?"

Andy walked away with a sly grin on his face, and yelled over his shoulder, "What do you think?"

Jesse ran a few steps to catch up to him. "I've got all winter to practice...if you have spare bullets. I'll pay you back for them. A man should learn how to use a gun."

"Well, that depends," Andy lectured with fatherly advice ."Some hands would've been better for never having touching one. Guns are like money, son. They give people a sense of power. Some folks can handle power. Some can't. Simple as that."

They continued towards the barn. "I think I could handle power," Jesse said honestly with a serious face.

Andy glanced over at the young man, amused at his self-confidence. "We'll see."

4

Winter between the timberline and foothills encompassed the little homestead earlier than the lower valley, secluding the farm for the season. With all supplies carefully bought and now rationed to last the winter months, one might have thought that life settled down to a fairly uneventful existence in the Kaleb household. But with Jesse's young spirit, the house came alive with chatter and laughter and zestful games of checkers and cards. Caroline spun yarn from goat hair and sheep's wool to knit socks and liners for their leather mitts. Andy's fiddle music entertained the evenings along with Caroline's determination that Jesse should become more worldly by reading aloud one chapter every evening from a book of her choosing.

Caroline's father had been a teacher. Both her parents were killed on a wagon train heading for the west to start up a new school and library. They had left Caroline with an Aunt until they were settled, but she never saw them again. Their horses had stampeded and tipped the wagon over a steep cliff, plunging all to their death. As a fourteen year old, Caroline inherited little, other than an old trunk full of books, but she remembered how her father prized them and so she did, as well.

There were books on every topic one might think a library to possess; Science, History, Astronomy, Politics, Finance, Shakespeare, Veterinary, Horticulture. At first, Jesse had been reluctant to take part in the reading, but he knew he owed Caroline big for the care she had given him, and so he obliged. After a month, he became thirsty for the knowledge in the books, and long after he had finished reading his one chapter aloud to her, he would settle in a quiet corner of the room with a candle, and continue reading on his own. Caroline would sneak a peek over at him once in awhile and smile to herself, thinking how pleased her parents would have been to see their books read by a promising young mind.

One morning after breakfast, Jesse slapped a book down on the table with excited gusto. His eyes were dancing with the prospect of copying a blueprint from the book. "We could improvise on this design in here. We have plenty of logs and..."

"Whoa," Andy interrupted, putting one hand over the pages of the book to conceal their information. "What castle are you planning to build? We ain't royalty here."

"Don't discourage the boy, Andy," Caroline scolded softly. "Let him tell you his plans."

"We could add a room on the north side of the house with..."

"More room to have to heat come winter," Andy cut in negatively. "Too much to heat as it is...or I'll be havin' to cut down half the mountainside."

"Well, then, we could fix the east side of the barn where that side is leaning ov..."

"Has Caroline been feeding you too many cinnamon buns again? If you touch that wall, it'll buckle clean on top of you. Too far gone to fix. The weight of a heavy snowfall on the roof a few years back buckled the beams inside. Gonna have to let it fall, then pick up the pieces. You stay away from that side of the barn or it'll bury ya."

Jesse's face fell and the excitement died in his eyes." Just a thought," he said quietly. "I'm ...good with a hammer. Not with a gun, but...I'm good with a hammer."

"Is that so?" Andy squinted his eyes and tilted his head slightly sideways to examine Jesse's dejected face. "You're right. You're no gunfighter, that's for sure...and you're definitely not a gambler from the way you play cards. You'll owe me a year's wages by spring if we keep playing cards...Okay, let me see those plans again."

Jesse flipped the pages to a second blueprint, and as Jesse explained the diagram with alterations of his own, Andy became quietly enthralled by the young man's knowledge on the subject of construction.

By the time the snow started to melt in little rivulets across the yard and green boughs poked their pine needles through crusty layers of ice, the Kaleb farmyard had taken on rebirth. The broken corral fences were now mended. The barn, once leaning dangerously to the east, was now standing square and sturdy with a new support wall. The house expansion had not happened, but the window glass was finally tight in its frame and a fine, wooden kitchen cabinet was standing in a corner of the room, holding Caroline's prized china. The cabinet had been made by a skilled hand with little tools to work with, and yet, the end result amazed both Andy and Caroline.

"You were right," Andy expressed, running his hands over the smooth, polished finish of the cabinet that Jesse had made for Caroline. "You're good with a hammer."

"Wait until Madison sees it," Caroline beamed. "She won't believe you made it."

A frown wrinkled Jesse's forehead. "Who's Madison?"

Before Andy could open his mouth to mention she was the daughter of someone in the valley, Caroline blurted out, "Your bride some day."

Jesse's eyebrows arched and he looked at Andy in bewilderment.

Andy came quickly to his rescue. "Caroline, now don't you go trying to marry the boy off before he's seen half the girls in the valley". He let out a hearty laugh to make light of the situation. "Women are always trying to play match-maker."

"Those other girls are wishy-washy compared to Madison," Caroline informed them both strongly with hands on her hips. "She can shoot a pea out of a pod at 50 feet."

"Oh, I'll for sure marry her, knowing that," Jesse said wryly, "...seeing as I'm useless with a gun. She likely plays poker with the best of them too." In his mind, Jesse quickly visioned Madison Graham as a burly hunk of a woman who could shot and play cards and spit with the best of the men.

"Well, got to finish that gate before your goats discover there's a hole in it," he quickly announced, and scooted towards the door before Caroline had any more wedding plans for him.

Caroline added as he reached the door, "You know, she still rides Timber, your mountain horse."

Jesse turned around very slowly, his hand resting on the doorknob. "Well now. She has my horse too. Guess I'm going to have to marry her just to get my things back." He stepped out onto the veranda and shut the door gently behind him. Then he laughed out loud and shook his head. He was never quite ready for the surprises that Caroline sprung on him.

ଓଷ୍ଠ

Madison had waited anxiously all winter for spring to arrive. She now watched buds on the trees pop open with lime green leaves, and birds bustle about building nests in their branches. She knew snow would soon disappear from the mountain slopes, making the trail to the Kalebs possible again.

In April, Madison started working in the Northfork bank as a teller, but her thoughts were in the mountains. She had made peace with Troy, mostly because he was her brother's best friend. However, she no longer dated the young man, despite his persistence. The reason was not because of Troy's deception. It was because she could not shake off the stories about Jesse and the excitement in her heart when she visioned him alive. It was like cheating on Troy with a ghost.

Madison's father was observant and noticed his daughter's glances towards the mountains whenever she thought nobody was watching. Mel Graham felt it was only a matter of time before his daughter would try to slip away to visit the Kalebs again. He finally approached her with a safer proposition. "We finished smoking pork this week, and it might be nice if you took a slab of bacon and a ham up to Andy and Caroline Kaleb. Timothy, of course, will accompany you. You can leave at dawn tomorrow morning. It should take you about three hours to get there...and I want you both home long before dark. Timothy has chores. Understood?"

Madison nodded, trying not to show too much jubilance in case her father thought her possessed with seeing the Kalebs. She was apprehensive to bring Timothy, not because he wasn't good company, but because she feared he might think Caroline strange and ruin their visit. Madison had looked forward to this visit all winter, but now she wasn't sure how to speak to Caroline in front of her brother. She couldn't pretend Jesse was alive with Timothy present. He would think she was nuts.

"All I ask is that you be nice, no matter what she says about Jesse," Madison warned her brother. His laugher in reply was an uncommitted answer.

Timothy and Madison reached the Kaleb homestead before noon, and Madison's mouth dropped open at the change in the farmyard. "Is there something wrong?" Timothy questioned the shocked look on her face.

"No! No!," she said cheerfully, trying to act as if everything was perfectly normal. "I had just forgotten how beautiful it is here with the pines and mountains towering behind the buildings." Her eyes darted about the yard, observing all the changes. She could not vision Andy capable of doing it alone.

They tied their horses to the railing outside the house, and Madison called loudly, "Mrs.Kaleb. Are you there? It's Madison...Hello!"

The front door swung open and Caroline fairly flew off the steps and into Madison's arms. "It's so good to see you, child. I'm so sorry. You've missed Jesse again. They left early this morning to go to Northfork for supplies. I'm surprised you didn't meet them on the trail. Oh never you mind. They must have taken a detour around by the beaver dam. Come in! Come in!"

Suddenly, Caroline noticed Madison's brother standing beside their horses, and she froze at the sight of him. After a long moment of silence, Caroline's voice escaped with a whisper. "Timothy? Is that you, Timothy?" She had not see him since before Jesse's death.

He nodded and a soft sigh relaxed her body. "Little Timmy. Oh my! You've grown into a man...but of course you have...of course you have...Jesse's older than you and he's all grown up too."

Timothy glanced awkwardly at Madison, begging her to rescue him. He didn't know what to say in response.

"We brought you some bacon and ham," Caroline cut in. "We finished smoking this week and thought you might like some." She took the parcels of wrapped meat out of her saddlebag and handed them to Caroline.

Caroline held the bacon package close to her nose for a whiff of the hickory-smoked pork. "Mmmmm! Delicious! Andy and Jesse are going to love this with eggs tomorrow morning. Come to think of it, Jesse will likely get into it before tomorrow morning, so I better hide it and keep it cool." Caroline and Madison laughed heartily together, while Timothy eyed them suspiciously, thinking to himself that both women were a little off their rockers.

"Come in for tea and some fresh biscuits," Caroline called back to Timothy, as she mounted the veranda steps with her arms around Madison's waist. Timothy didn't have to wait for a second invitation to food. Once inside the house, Madison couldn't take her eyes off the beautiful kitchen cabinet. Caroline handed Timothy a cup of tea and said, "Tell me what you've been doing, Timothy Graham."

"I'd rather have you tell me what Jesse's been doing," Timothy answered back, stuffing a warm biscuit with honey into his mouth. Madison threw him a nasty scowl.

"Well, for starters," Caroline exploded with any chance to talk about Jesse, "I have this new kitchen cabinet for my china. Now isn't that the most beautiful thing you've ever seen?"

"I've been admiring it since I walked in the door," Madison confessed. "It's beautifully made .How did you get it all the way up here into the mountains without scratching it?"

"Jesse made it."

The cabin was so silent; one could hear the call of a blue jay far on the timberline. Finally, Madison blurted out. "Jesse made it? Oh, tell him I would love a little chest with horses galloping all around the outside and an oval in the middle with a horse head and a girl carved on it." Then Madison grinned mischievously and patted Caroline's shoulder. "Just joking! The cabinet is beautiful. I see your barn is fixed too."

"And finally that dang window is solid in the frame and has quit whistling at me every time the wind blows." Caroline laughed. "He's going to make me a bookcase next. He says books shouldn't be kept in a trunk or they'll smell like unwashed socks."

"He can read?" Timothy blurted out spontaneously, recalling Troy's perception of Jesse being only able to talk in grunts. Madison threw him a look that could kill, so he quickly amended his manners. "I mean...him not going to school and all."

Madison hastily changed the subject by jumping up to admire Caroline's delicate china in the cabinet. "You have such beautiful china, Mrs. Kaleb. The pattern is so unique with the violets."

"My Aunt left the dish set to me when she died. She said every lady needs something frivolous. I kept it safe in a chest for years without putting it out. Why do people do that? How foolish to hide something so beautiful." Caroline held a cup tenderly to her chest and closed her eyes, remembering a special Aunt from long ago. "She was a mother and guardian angel to me after my parents were killed."

Caroline suddenly threw her arms up in the air like an excited child. "Come see my flowerbed. The hollyhocks are just beginning to peep through the ground." The women scurried off like busy squirrels to investigate the garden. Timothy decided to stay behind, closer to the biscuits and honey.

Time flew by for the women, as Caroline delighted in showing all her gardens and farmyard animals to Madison. Finally, Timothy interrupted their visitation. "Time to go, Madison. Father says we must be back early."

Caroline hugged each of the young people before they left. "Thanks for the bacon and ham and for your visit. You both come back."

Timothy nodded, while Madison ran back and hugged Caroline one more time.

Slowly, their horses wound down the mountain, passing through streams fringed with towering pine. Madison didn't say anything. She was waiting for Timothy to make the first remark, but he remained silent for so long, she finally spoke up. "Someone made that cabinet and I don't think Andy Kaleb's hands have the skill, do you?"

"Don't you go spooking me, sis. Once we get down out of these mountains, and back into my territory, that's okay, but not now. I don't need no spirit creeping up on me way out here in the wilderness."

"You honestly look a little green in the face, Tim. Are you thinking Jesse's still alive too?"

"No, I'm not," he insisted strongly. But at the same time, Timothy flung a quick look over his shoulder to make sure a ghost wasn't following him.

5

Andy and Jesse informed Caroline that they needed supplies in Northfork, but instead, they left early for Riverflats, a town further south of Northfork; the only other town in the valley before having to cross the mountain chain. As promised, Andy was taking Jesse to another locality to see if they could find out his identity.

On route, the men stopped a short time to rest their horses. Andy took out a pipe and puffed a few rings of smoke while Jesse stretched his youthful body upon a large flat rock, which had been warmed from the morning sun. Jesse looked up at the sky, and finally confessed to Andy, "I've been remembering a few more things...but I'm not sure they'll please you."

"What other things?" Andy asked, taking his pipe slowly from his mouth, a worried look clouding his eyes.

Jesse explained, "At first, I recalled a gun being forced into my hand and a man insisting I avenge someone's death. That's all I could remember for a long time. I should have said something, but I tried out your pistols to see if I was any good with a gun, and as you know, I wasn't, so I'm for sure no gunfighter. Now, bits and pieces of other things are coming back to me. I remember this big man. He used to push me around a lot...not a nice fellow. I think he's the one who put the gun in my hand."

"Can you remember anyone else... father... mother... wife..?"

"Only a man with a black moustache standing between me and the big man. I must have been young because I wasn't able to see over his shoulder. I remember resting my cheek against his back and feeling my tears wet his shirt. The big fellow had something in his hand...I'm sure he was going to hit me with it...but the man with the moustache wouldn't let him."

"Sounds like something a father would do...protect his kid," Andy said thoughtfully. "Can you remember anything else?"

Jesse shook his head negatively. "Not much. I do remember standing alone on a hilltop, trying to straighten a crooked cross in the ground. There was no one else standing beside me...just that big man sitting in a wagon a distance away, yelling at me to get my butt moving. I kept looking back at that crooked cross as we drove away, thinking the deceased person would be disappointed that I didn't get the cross pounded in straight."

Jesse slid down from the rock and tightened the cinch on his saddle. He mounted his horse, ready to ride again. "Do you think I went out and killed someone? Perhaps I was hiding in the mountains when I arrived at your place."

"Guess that's what we're here to find out." Andy said, trying to calm Jesse's concern. "Let's first see if anyone recognizes you in Riverflats."

"Maybe stop at the sheriff 's office first," Jesse advised. "Make sure I'm not wanted and us gunned down or something. I don't want to get you into any trouble."

Andy and Jesse rode into Riverflats. Few people lifted their eyes, and none showed any interest or recognition of Jesse. Their first destination was the sheriff's office and as they mounted the boardwalk, both Andy and Jesse's stomachs grumbled from nervousness.

The sheriff rose from behind his desk and asked what he could do for the two strangers who timidly entered his office. Jesse proceeded to explain that he had suffered memory loss due to a head injury, and was hoping the sheriff might help him piece the puzzle together.

The sheriff's eyes gradually squinted as Jesse explained his situation. The lawman traced every feature of Jesse's face. Suddenly, he reached out his hand for a handshake. "Gil. Gracious, it is you. You've grown some. I never recognized you there for a while. It's gotta be more than a dozen years ago or so."

Jesse stared blankly at the sheriff, desperately trying to find some small recognizable feature, but nothing surfaced. He returned the sheriff's handshake out of politeness.

Andy spoke up. "He doesn't remember much. What can you tell him about his family...and some big man who told him to avenge a death."

"That would be Harry Rideau...your father's brother and partner in the furniture business. After your father's death, you was sent back east to your Aunt Krystaline and Harry ran the business until his drinking got the best of him. Lost everything. Still living in a shack down by the river. Does odd jobs to feed himself and buy booze."

The sheriff shook his head with regret and continued, "Your father used to run a pretty good business when he was alive. Guilbert owned seventy-five percent of it, and as long as he managed the place, he could keep Harry sober enough to put in half a day's work. Once Guilbert was gone, Harry never stayed sober long enough to nail an egg crate together. Sorry to say he drank the business away."

"I mostly remember Harry being nasty to me. Can't remember why," Jesse mentioned in puzzlement.

"Well, I know the answer to that," the sheriff said with a compassionate sigh."Guilbert found out he had a terminal illness, so went back east to tell his sister, Krystaline in Boston. While there, he ran into you, sitting in the rain like a wet rag of a cat. Seems you ran away from some orphanage, so he brought you home and called you his "Little Gil". Guess he kinda wanted someone to take his place after he was gone, and likely someone to watch over Harry. Guilbert lasted another two and a half years before he died."

The sheriff walked over to the office window and peered out onto the street, a habit he had incurred from years of checking for trouble. Seeing all at peace in the streets, he returned to speak to Jesse. "Harry near to took a fit when his brother brought you back, and an even bigger fit when he found out Guilbert had put you heir to his seventy-five percent of the business. After Harry found out about Guilbert's will, he drank double, and Harry was a mean man when he drank."

"I kind of remember that part," Jesse said somewhat under his breath, remembering slaps across the face and bruised arms from being grabbed and tossed aside. "I need to see him anyway. Can you give me directons to his shack?...Oh, and do you know who this person is that Harry wanted me to avenge?"

"Likely your father. Far as anyone knows, some thief came in, clubbed Guilbert on the head and killed him with one blow. The person responsible was never found."

"I thought he died of a terminal illness," Jesse frowned.

"Would have," the sheriff said, shaking his head in sorrow. "Killed before the illness got him."

As Jesse turned to leave, the sheriff added a word of comfort. "Guilbert thought the world of you, boy. Brought you here to give you a better life. He knew Harry wasn't capable of running the place with his booze problem, and hoped you'd keep the business going for both of your sakes. That's why he willed you his share of the business. Of course, there's no business left for you now, but his intentions were good...Say, wait a minute!"

The sheriff disappeared for a few minutes and then came back with a square wooden chest in his hands. He blew the dust off the top of the chest and polished the lid with his elbow before handing it to Jesse. "Harry was selling stuff off a few years ago for whiskey and I bought this. Used to be Guilbert's. Thought maybe in my old age, I'd take up whittlin' with these fancy blades, but never found the time. Take 'em. Guilbert would want you to have them." He opened the box to reveal eighteen keen-edged carving tools neatly displayed in the wooden case.

"I'll pay for them," Jesse stated, but the sheriff shook his head in refusal.

"My tribute to Guilbert. I can see by lookin' at ya that he'd be mighty proud of what you growed into."

Jesse nodded thanks and exited quietly with the chest. He tied it securely to his saddle and followed the sheriff's directions to a shack beside the river. The shack was surrounded by years of dead, uncut weeds, which concealed the windows like a shaggy beige curtain. A huge man rocked in an old armchair on the front porch, a whiskey bottle in one hand and a dirty handkerchief in the other. He wiped his brow as Jesse dismounted and approached him.

"Remember me?" Jesse asked. "Gil."

Harry's bloodshot eyes opened wide and his voice escaped in a drunken slur. "So, you've growed up and come back to get the business, have ya? Well, you'll not get so much as a nail from it. I seen to that." His ruddy unshaven cheeks grew increasingly red as blood rushed to his face in excitement. He had waited years for this moment.

"There was no need of it, ya know." Harry spat close to Jesse's boots. "We was doing good...then he dragged you out of some alley and made you lord and master over me...his own brother? Can you believe that?"

Jesse didn't reply to his ramblings." You gave me a gun, Harry. Why not avenge your brother's death yourself? What did you expect a child to do?"

Harry looked up at the young man standing tall and strong above him. "Wanted to throw you back in the streets where you come from, but Krystaline insisted on taking you after Guilbert was gone. She died of smallpox a couple years later. Didn't know what happened to you after that. Didn't know and didn't care...Still don't."

Jesse's eyes narrowed with distaste.

Harry blew his nose in his handkerchief and laughed wickedly. "I knowed they'd hang you someday for it. Thief, that's what you was...nothing more than a horse thief." He blew his nose again. "I knowed you'd figure it out when you was growed." Harry went to tip the whiskey bottle to his lips again. Jesse yanked it out of his hands and sat the bottle upright in the grass several feet away. Harry reached out a grappling hand to retrieve the bottle, but was incapable of getting up in his drunken state.

Jesse impatiently gave the man's boot a kick." What was I supposed to figure out?"

Harry laughed. "That I was the one that done it, boy. That I was the one who done it to stop you from getting what wasn't yours. He was dyin' anyway. Be gone in a year. Then there you'd be, standing there in your polished boots, telling me to do this and to do that for the rest of my life... well, not in a pig's eye. I seen to that. Knew you'd figure it out someday and come back gunning me fer it. Been waiting."

Jesse's face turned white and he stood speechless. Harry's bloodshot eyes looked up at him, waiting like a snake to strike and destroy Jesse any way that he could, even at the sacrifice of his own life.

"Are you telling me you clubbed your own brother to death, so I'd kill you in revenge and hang for it? " Jesse could not believe the depth of Harry's hate for him. "You did that...simply over shares in a business? I would have given it all to you if you had asked. What kind of a brother are you?"

Harry laughed through tobacco stained teeth, hoping to pull Jesse into his twisted scheme. "Yellow-bellied little snip. That's all you are," he taunted. "You haven't got the guts to do what's right by your Pa, do you."

Jesse slowly walked over to the whiskey bottle and plucked it out of the grass. He calmly sat the bottle back in Harry's shaking hands. "I don't want anything from you, Harry, not even this stinking bottle. I never did." Then he turned quietly to Andy. "Let's get out of here." His stomach felt like a rock had settled in the bottom of it.

Jesse threw his leg over the saddle, and yelled down at the drunken man. "Rot in hell by yourself, Uncle." Jesse whirled his horse about and galloped quickly away from the river. Cursing words fell upon the young man's back, but he merely tightened his fist around the reins and rode on without looking back.

As he was leaving Riverflats, Jesse's eyes drifted toward the cemetery on the hillside, and he swung his horse in that direction. On the hillside, he walked from cross to cross until he recognized one leaning strongly to the right. He picked up a large rock and used it as a hammer to straighten the cross.

"It's about time I straightened that, eh father." He patted the cross with an affectionate hand, and then turned towards Andy, who waited a respectful distance away with Jesse's horse.

"You going to tell the sheriff?" Andy asked quietly, as he watched Jesse mount his chestnut gelding.

Jesse shook his head sadly and sighed. "Wouldn't change much after all these years. Can't bring Guilbert back...and I reckon Harry's harmless to anyone else except me. Likely the best punishment for him is to sit and think about what he did for the rest of his life."

They rode a long while in silence. Andy thought it best to let Jesse digest what had happened before he said anything to him.

Finally, Andy spoke up. "You know, your father did leave you an inheritance...not material, but in the couple years you were with him, he must have taught you a lot about wood working. Furniture like you made for Caroline would sell for a lot down in the valley."

Jesse looked at his hands. "Guess that's why I'm good with a hammer." His eyes shone with the revelation.

"Ya well, don't get too cocky, 'cause you're worthless with a gun," Andy quipped good-naturedly. "But...if you were good with a gun...you'd be okay with the power. You proved that today."

Jesse nodded a quiet thank you in return. After awhile, Jesse turned to Andy with a gentle, tired smile. "Bet mother's got cinnamon buns waiting for me."

Andy smiled back. "Yes, I'll bet she has."

6

It was two months before Madison had spare time to ride as far into the mountains as Runaway River again, where she had first met Caroline fishing. "It's a great fishing hole," she explained to her father. "Fish fry tonight if I catch any...and don't tell Timothy to come with me. All he does is skim pebbles across the stream and scare the fish."

Her father sighed with resignation, knowing it was impossible to refuse a meal of fresh fish from the mountain stream. "Three hours. That's it, and then we come looking for you...and take my shotgun...better than a revolver in case of bear. Charlie Hopkins said he saw a bear up by his far quarter last week near Runaway River, so keep an eye out."

Madison swung her legs over her mountain horse, and tucked her fishing rod and the shotgun beside her leg. Madison's mother came out of the house just as she was about to ride away. Madison turned and waved to her, then galloped towards the mountains before her father changed his mind.

Loretta Graham turned to her husband with raised eyebrows. "You realize she's hoping to see Caroline at the fishing hole again, don't you?"

Mel nodded. "I know, but she's grown up now. Half the girls in the valley are married at her age. We can't keep her in a cradle forever."

"Yes, but it would be nice," Loretta sighed. "She's a little too adventurous...like her father."

Timothy had been fixing a hitch on a wagon. He lay down his tools and walked across the farmyard towards his parents when he saw Madison gallop out of the yard. "I thought come spring, she'd get over this foolishness," Timothy stated strongly, "but she's still got it into her head that Jesse is alive, and I blame Andy Kaleb a lot for that. He fuels his wife's fantasy. He's obviously gone to Riverflats and brought back that cabinet for his wife, and pretended Jesse made it. He can mislead his wife all he wants, but he better stop misleading Madison before the whole valley thinks my sister is as nutty as an oak tree. Something needs to be done about it."

"Your sister is no fool. She knows the truth," Mel deliberated. "She's just wrapped up in an adventure of sorts. Let her figure it out."

Timothy shrugged and turned to go back to his work. He yelled over his shoulder, "Well, let's hope she doesn't come home telling us she's marrying the phantom, 'cause I'm not being best man to an invisible groom."

Mel and Loretta laughed, but inwardly, they felt no humor in the situation, as they too, were concerned over Madison's obsession with the deceased Jesse Kaleb.

Madison climbed upward along the small trail that wound between the rocks and pines, her mountain horse ever sure-footed and mindful of the terrain. As she passed by the falls, which dropped down into a lake and then narrowed to form Runaway River, she thought for a moment that she saw a rider high on the cliffs above the falls, watching her pass below. She halted Timber to get a more focused view, but when she glanced upwards again, the rider was gone. She wondered if she had imagined it, for as much as she enjoyed pretending Jesse lived, deep in her mind, she knew him to be a fantasy.

Madison rounded the last grove of pines on the hillside and broke into a smile to find Caroline fishing once again at the river with her two coonhounds sleeping nearby. Caroline turned to watch Madison approach, an expression of delight crossing her face from one rosy cheek to the other.

"How's the fishing?" Madison called to Caroline, as she dismounted and carried her gear to the edge of the stream. Madison flung her line into the stream and sat down on a rock beside Caroline.

"Jesse caught two about an hour ago," Caroline answered with pride, "but he promised to help his Pa with some planting, so couldn't stay long. I'm surprised you didn't run into him going home." She stood up and recast her line.

The women fished side by side until Caroline suddenly remembered a parcel in her saddlebag. She retrieved the parcel and handed it to Madison. "I've been carrying this around all spring, hoping I'd see you somewhere. Jesse made it for you."

In surprise, Madison graciously accepted the gift, and carefully unwrapped the washed flour sack from around the article. Her mouth dropped open at the sight of a beautiful wooden chest. A herd of galloping horses was carved around the entire sides of the chest with an oval in the centre of the lid, portraying a girl's face leaning against a horse head. The horse's head showed a distinct evergreen star on its forehead. It was carved exactly as she had described to Caroline, and for several minutes, Madison could barely catch her breath. Finally she blurted, "I...I have never owned anything so beautiful. It's almost magical...How can I ever thank him?"

"Jesse says you can return his horse," Caroline smiled with a twinkle in her eye. Madison looked up in shock, so Caroline laughed. "Oh, he's just kidding. Of course, he won't take his horse back. He knows how much you love Timber. He's such a rascal."

Madison traced her fingers over the horse carvings. "I can't believe someone could do this. It's so perfect, like a photograph carved in wood." She turned the chest over in her hands, admiring all the details. When she glanced at the bottom, she noted a short carved message, which read, "From Jesse and Timber."

Madison started to laugh. "I think he's trying to bribe me into giving his horse back."

Madison showed Caroline the message on the bottom of the carved chest, and Caroline shook her head in disgust. "I'm going to have to scold the boy about that."

"I wish I could thank him in person, but father said I must be back soon, or he'll come looking for me."

After awhile, Caroline suddenly tossed her straw hat at her sleeping coonhounds, "Wake up, you silly guard dogs. Time to get home. If I'm not back, Jesse will for sure try to start lunch, and boil potatoes in the pee-pot."

Madison laughed out loud at Caroline's humor. "Tell him I said thank you...the chest is unbelievable."

As Madison returned home, she passed once again at the base of the falls. She glanced upward and wondered if there was some way she could climb to the top of the falls and check for hoof prints. She tied Timber to a tree, and proceeded to climb the face of the cliffs, carefully implanting her toes in crevices to hoist herself upwards. Once at the top, she walked about the ground, looking for evidence that a rider had been there. The ground was solid rock close to the water flow, so no tracks could be detected. She walked further afield, ever widening her circle of investigation until she noticed the trace of hoof prints in looser soil. A little gasp escaped her lips.

Caroline had mentioned Jesse leaving her earlier. Could the ghost of Jesse actually exist in these mountains? Had he been watching her from this spot at the top of the falls? She shivered at the thought, half excited and half fearful of a creature believed dead by the valley.

☙❧

The morning did not hold peace for Madison. When she revealed the carved chest to her family, Timothy was enraged. He insisted Andy had bought the chest in Riverflats, just as he had probably done with the cabinet. Madison argued back that Timothy had witnessed her telling Caroline exactly what she would like carved on the chest, so it was too much of a coincidence. "And the horse carved on the front has Timber's evergreen star," she explained. "It had to be made for me."

Timothy frowned deeply. "It's eery, and I don't like it. They need to confess to what is going on. We all know Jesse is dead. You better stay down here in the valley, or I'm paying them a visit." He figured maybe blackmail was the only thing that would keep his sister safely out of the mountains.

"It's none of our business what they want to believe. They're not harming anyone," Madison argued." You'll just upset Caroline if you start questioning her."

Madison turned to her parents for moral support, but they agreed with Timothy. "It's best you stay out of the mountains until we know who really made you the chest, dear," Loretta soothed in a gentle tone. "Obviously something is not exactly normal up there. Caroline probably told Andy about what you wanted carved on a chest, and he likely had the chest made for you in Riverflats. Maybe he does these things all the time to keep Caroline happy. I'm sure Andy means no harm, but he shouldn't drag you into their fantasies. Let your father speak to Andy about it before you visit them again. If Andy's explanation is fine with your father, then it shouldn't harm you to visit them once in awhile." Loretta turned to her son with a firm eye, "...and no one is going to approach Caroline. That woman has suffered enough."

Madison squared her shoulders and picked up the chest. "Andy would never have the money to buy such things, and no one in Riverflats or Northfork can carve like this or we'd know about it."

"It's rather ghostly," Timothy snorted. "Almost scares me to look at it."

"Well, I LOVE it," Madison replied and returned her prized possession to her bedroom before Timothy got some weird idea to destroy it.

Come late evening, Madison was restless and decided to hit for the corral to groom Timber. As she picked up a bucket and brushes in the feed room, she overheard voices coming from a nearby stall. She sat the pail down quietly and kept to the shadows as she inched her way closer to the stall to see who was talking. It puzzled her that anyone would be in the barn at this time of night.

Timothy's voice whispered clear enough for her to comprehend. "We'll meet tomorrow at midnight. They should all be in bed by then. It'll take us until three o'clock to get there, snoop around a bit and see who is there, and then get back by six or seven."

Troy's voice cut in. "We'd best leave a note on our beds that we've gone hunting tomorrow morning or something, 'cause our folks will be up long before six and wonder where we are."

"Good idea! I just want to see if someone else is up there besides Andy and Caroline Kaleb," Timothy explained. "I noticed things were fixed up in the yard, things that Andy couldn't do by himself. Looks suspicious...like someone has moved in."

"Yeah!" Troy agreed, "He'll likely shove them down the well when he's got no more use for them. We'll wait until he has to go to the outhouse, then grab him and make him spill the truth of what's going on."

"Well, we don't want any rough stuff, 'cause we'll be trespassing and they have the right to fill our butts full of lead. I heard Father say once that Andy was a gunslinger in his younger days and could shoot you faster than a wink. Best not to be seen. Could be Andy is back associating with gun fighters again. Maybe someone is using his place as a hideout."

Troy shifted his footing a bit. "Makes sense. Well, then we'll just scout them out from a distance. Bring your telescope. I gotta see this Jesse Kaleb in the flesh...or whatever ghostly form he's in."

"Don't mention ghosts," Timothy shivered. "Can't stand the thought of ghosts, but we gotta do something, 'cause this carved chest is the last straw. They're messing with Maddy's mind and we've gotta stop them."

Madison quietly slipped back into the tack room and then sat down to deliberate on what she should do. She had to warn the Kalebs, partly to protect Caroline's belief in Jesse, but mostly because she was afraid Andy Kaleb might think her brother and Troy were wild animals hanging about the yard and shoot them. Even if she informed her parents of their plan and stopped them this time, the boys would probably try another night. She had promised herself not to lie to her parents again, but this was an emergency. The boy's lives depended on it.

Early the next morning, Madison stuffed a pair of riding pants into a bag, and dressed in a long skirt for work at the bank. She popped into the kitchen with a cheery smile and greeted her mother, who was preparing pancakes for the family breakfast. "I thought you had Friday off," her mother exclaimed, surprised to see Madison dressed in her work attire.

"Oh, I thought I told you that I had to work at the bank today. Extra big payrolls coming in, so I may be a bit late getting home. I'll not take the wagon this morning. Timber needs a shoe looked at, so I'll drop him off at the Blacksmiths for the day while I work." She swallowed a glass of milk, grabbed a couple pancakes and hit for the door before anyone could ask questions. At the door entrance, she grabbed her father's shotgun and a handful of shells from the closet, wrapped her shawl around them so no one would notice, and exited the house.

Once out of view, Madison leapt from her horse, and quickly changed from her skirt into riding pants. She remounted Timber, and set the shotgun by her leg, ready for easy and sudden use. Time was of the essence and so she rode swiftly in the direction of the mountains. As she rode, her heart was heavy, for she knew that lies destroy trust, and deeply regretted having to lie to her parents once again.

7

Jesse enjoyed riding along the ridge where he could look across the entire mountain chain and drink in the beauty of mountain peaks reflected in stream-fed lakes below. The scenery and fresh crisp air made him feel alive and based, as if his roots were gradually taking hold of something. At the same time, he felt guilty that he had not earned the right to feel as he did, for he was living a lie as Jesse Kaleb.

For a while, he relaxed his attentiveness to the forest around him, which is not wise in a terrain laced with the unforeseen. Halfway down the ridge, Jesse's horse bolted, and threw him roughly to the rocky ground before he had time control the horse and tighten his leg grip to the saddle. He was stunned and pushed himself slowly and stiffly to his feet, somewhat angry with himself for not being prepared for trouble. He looked around for Redtip, but his flighty chestnut was long gone. In the horse's place, stood a large black bear, raised on hind legs in challenge, looking straight at Jesse with cold, unwavering eyes. Jesse's horse had delivered him practically in the bear's lap.

Jesse swallowed. The rifle was in the scabbard on his saddle, and that was gone with the frightened horse. All he had for defense was a handgun in his gun belt. By the size of the bear, Jesse calculated that a bullet from his revolver would do little harm to the bear unless he aimed perfectly. But what should he aim at? Between the bear's eyes? Its heart? Exactly where was the bear's heart in such a massive black wall of fur? He didn't know. He wasn't a hunter. The bear approached closer, letting out a growl that forced Jesse's footsteps backward until his back rested against a tree. He glanced upward. Should he try to climb the tree? No time...Anyhow, black bears could also climb trees, couldn't they? His mind was whirling. Where could he run to?...No, they say not to run. That only stimulates a wild animal to attack even more. What was left then? The bear was almost on him. Jesse's shaky hands gripped the revolver as he tried to remember everything Andy told him about aiming straight and true.

"Boom!" The sound of a shotgun echoed through the air, and the bear froze, took a few steps backward, then collapsed at Jesse's feet. Jesse had not fired his revolver. He turned around slowly to see Madison sitting calmly upon her horse with her shotgun raised, smoke still curling from its long barrel. Madison slowly lowered her gun. Was this Jesse in the flesh, as real as the bear who had almost killed him...or a stranger passing this way? She studied him more closely, half hoping he was Jesse, and half hoping he was not, for she knew Jesse to be dead.

"I had him in my sights," Jesse uttered feebly, embarrassed that a young lady should have to rescue him.

"Looked like he had you in HIS sights...from where I sat," Madison answered smugly, and Jesse lowered his face with a little grin, knowing she spoke the truth.

"Well, if I'd had MY horse," Jesse lifted his chin again, glancing up at Timber who was standing quietly in front of him, undaunted by the sight of the bear or the sound of the gun, "I wouldn't have been ditched at the sight of a bear."

Madison gasped slightly. If he knew Timber had once been his horse, then he must be Jesse. She didn't know what to say. She looked at the bear and knew Andy sold a few furs. She blurted out, "Are you going to skin him?"

Jesse glanced at the bear. He had no clue how to skin a bear, and he really had no desire to learn, but he didn't want Madison to know that. In fact, he had to be careful with everything he said if he was to continue his masquerade as Andy and Caroline's son. Until the time came when Caroline accepted him as someone other than Jesse, he was not going to destroy her fantasy. He owed her that much for her kindness. "I'll get father to bring the wagon for the hide. I'm on foot at the moment."

Madison dismounted and walked over closer to the bear. She still carried her shotgun, and reloaded as she looked down at him. "I'll take you home. Timber can carry double. Man, that's a big bear, but...u-oh, I think he's still breathing...Step back...quick!"

The words had barely escaped her mouth when the bear rose in a flurry of clawing arms. His wide mouth growled as he attacked, blood dripping from long vicious teeth. Having been wounded, the bear's anger was now doubled. Madison stumbled backward and fell, the shotgun flying from her hands as she hit the ground. Jesse caught the shotgun in mid-air, and flung himself on the ground beside her, firing without hesitation square into the attacking bear's face. This time, the bear fell with a thunderous thud and did not move.

The close encounter with death solemned their moods. Madison and Jesse sat side by side in the grass, neither communicating with the other for a long time. Jesse slowly kicked the bear's limp arm off his leg and directed his attention to a dragonfly, which had landed on his knee, twitching its wings to master balance in the mountain breeze. Jesse watched the insect as if in a trance.

Meanwhile, a breeze feathered Madison's blond hair about the crown of her head, as she stared face down at the grass between her knees. Her focus was far from the encounter with the bear. Numbed, she watched several ants thread their way through the maze of grass blades and wondered where they were headed. Sometimes when death brushes so closely, time stands still for a short while. It is only when you notice the rise and fall of your chest, that you realize you are still alive...still breathing.

After a long silence, Jesse turned to her and reached out his hand for a handshake. "I'm Jesse."

Madison looked at his hand and received it timidly. Her hand was trembling, but she wasn't sure if it was from the close encounter with the bear or from the warmth of Jesse's touch. She half expected his hand to be ghostly cold, but Jesse's palm was warm and alive. "I'm Madison," she replied with a slight tremble in her voice.

"Nice to meet you," Jesse smiled, and scrambled to his feet, reaching out his hand to help her rise.

Madison looked at him more clearly, almost expecting him to fade away in a puff of smoke, but he was flesh and blood, and he had Caroline's grey-green eyes.

"I was on my way to see your father," Madison revealed with slight embarrassment, suddenly remembering the reason for her trip to the Kalebs. "My brother and his friend have a mind to sneak up here tonight and check on whether you exist or not."

Jesse's eyebrows arched in amusement. "On whether I exist or not?"

Madison continued with awkwardness, "Word in the valley is that you died twelve years ago in a flash flood, and the boys think you're either a phantom or some suspicious stranger up to no good. I know your father was a gunslinger long ago and I didn't want him to shoot their..."

"A gunslinger!" Jesse interrupted in shock. "Well, no wonder that devil could shoot so..." He halted his speech. After all, he should know such things about his own father. He shut his mouth quickly, and bent over to pick up the shotgun and hand it back to her. "Phantom of the Mountain, eh! I like the sound of that. Maybe it'll keep people clear of my business."

Timber stood close in the clearing and Madison summoned the horse with a sharp whistle. Jesse flung himself into the saddle and pulled her up behind him. She slipped her arms about his waist for support and felt him flinch at her touch. She wondered if she was the first girl who had ever been this close to Jesse Kaleb, seeing as he had lived his whole life secluded in the mountains.

The pair rode along the wildlife trails, climbing higher and higher into the mountains. Gradually, it occurred to her that she was alone in the mountains with a complete stranger. Perhaps her brother and Troy were right and he was a dangerous man claiming to be the deceased Jesse. She should not have trusted him so soon. Fantasies can create perfect people with no flaws, but a real live Jesse might not be so perfect.

Occasionally, Jesse stopped the horse for a rest and they gazed down on the beautiful valley scenery. He did not speak and Madison thought he must not be used to conversing with people, so she did not force him to talk. After an hour, Jesse pulled Timber to a stop and turned to Madison. "Time to give the horse a break." They both dismounted, and he led Timber to a mountain stream for a drink of water. Madison noticed Jesse was now limping slightly, and she thought it was probably from being bruised when thrown from his horse.

They rested upon some fallen logs. Jesse grabbed his leg and winced as he sat down, so Madison questioned him about the injury. He shrugged it off as nothing to worry about, but she noticed the thigh of his jeans were ripped and a bloody stain leaking slightly above the knee area. He insisted it was just a scratch, so she let him be.

Madison found it difficult to believe this young man could remain hidden in the mountains for near twelve years. Yet, here he was, sitting on a tree trunk in front of her, surrounded by the mountains and forest that must have hidden him all these years. It was easy to believe in him when he was a fantasy, as then she and Caroline could set a plate at the table for him and make excuses why he was late for the meal, but now he was real and probably capable of being a total rat. Living with a fantasy was so much easier, and never disappointing.

Suddenly, Madison thought of the chest he had made for her. "Thank you for carving the beautiful chest for me. You are very talented."

Jesse shrugged off the compliment with humility. "Yeah, well, my father taught..." Once again, he had to hide the truth of his past. He dared not reveal any association with Guilbert Rideau. Instead, Jesse hoped somewhere in his past Andy Kaleb might have whittled a simple pipe for himself. "My father taught me a little whittling."

Jesse tried not to make eye contact with Madison for he was sure her keen eyes would pick up on his lie. He rose to his feet quickly to retrieve Timber from the stream before she could question him further. Jesse did not think he should converse much with Madison for fear of revealing his true identity by mistake. He had not prepared himself for being investigated, and it was too easy to slip up.

They rode in silence for a short time until they happened upon Andy Kaleb hurrying down the trail on Skat, dragging Jesse's chestnut horse behind them. Andy's relieved face blossomed when he saw Jesse was alive and unharmed, for he had feared the worst when Jesse's horse returned home without him.

Madison peeked her head out from behind Jesse's back. "Hi, Mr. Kaleb. A bear frightened Jesse's horse, but he shot the bear...and..."

"Jesse shot a bear?" Andy eyes widened in surprise and with a sudden pinch of fatherly pride.

"Kind of...first her...then me. I'll explain later," Jesse said hastily, as he dismounted and swung up onto his own horse. "If you want the bear's hide, he's a-ways down the mountain over by the cliff face."

"I'm sorry to interrupt," Madison cut in with an anxious voice, knowing it was time she started her return homeward, "but I have to talk to you quickly about my brother and his friend." She proceeded to explain the situation to Andy. He listened quietly, rubbing his chin in thoughtfulness.

"Don't like to see the boys riding in the mountains after dark. That old cat hunts at night up here. Best you tell your folks about their plan, and stop the boys before they leave. I also don't want them around the farmyard upsetting Caroline. They'd scare her half to death if she spied them sneaking around in the dark. Wouldn't trust her for grabbing the rifle and shooting them herself."

Andy turned to Jesse. "For Madison's safety, guess there's nothing else you can do but take her back down to her farm. Don't like her riding that far by herself. Let them see you're alive. Maybe that'll stop their curiosity. You ready for that?"

Jesse thought for a moment. He wasn't ready for questions. He had almost slipped up several times with Madison. "No, I'm not ready. I'll take her down to the valley floor, but that's as far as I'll go."

Madison thought Jesse's reluctance to see people was because the young man had never left the mountains since childhood, and had likely grown up anti-social. "Just ride with me into my yard, let them see you, nod hello and then turn and ride out. No questions asked. Nothing else," Madison promised.

"Guess I owe you that much for saving my life," Jesse mustered reluctantly. "But just remember, you owe me back for saving yours."

"Agreed!" Madison promised, and they headed their horses back down the mountain towards the Graham farm in the valley, while Andy continued towards the ridge to skin the bear.

As the young couple wound down the mountain trail, Jesse tried to keep as silent as possible, for he was afraid of revealing his true identity to Madison. He could see strands of her hair shimmer like gold threads floating in the wind every time they passed from shadow into sunlight. He mused that the gun-toting Madison Graham was not quite as he had visioned her. He had not expected her to be so beautiful.

"How come you never come down into the valley?" Madison questioned suddenly. "Why did you stop coming with your father to our place to pick up grain in the fall?"

Jesse had to think quickly. "Mother didn't like being left alone." His heart was beating fast. He wished Madison would stop asking questions.

"It's not good for you to never have contact with people or a community. You'll turn into an old hermit in the mountains with a beard down to your knees, and someone will mistake and shoot you for a bear."

Jesse smiled at her negative prediction. "Most likely by you," he murmured with amusement, and Madison laughed back, thinking he had inherited Caroline's sense of humor.

"How's your leg?" Madison changed the subject, noticing that Jesse was increasingly favoring his leg as the day went on. "When we rest the horses at Runaway River, we'd better take a look at that wound. Did you hurt it falling from your horse?"

"No! Just a small swipe from the bear's claws. It's nothing."

"Looks like it's bled a bit. Better check it out and clean it. You don't want infection."

They dismounted their horses by Runaway River and Jesse limped over to a pile of rocks to sit down. He gingerly tried to fold the fabric of his pants back to get a better look at the injury. By now, the blood had dried and stuck the fabric to his wound, so he winced as he tried to loosen the two from each other.

Madison dipped her hat in the clear river water and brought it over to where Jesse sat. "If I pour some water on it, it may free the cloth." He nodded approval, so she gently poured water from her hat across his thigh. The ice-cold water made him tense in shock and grit his teeth.

"Sorry," she sympathized, and he glanced up into her eyes with pain evident on his face. Their faces were so close, Madison could count the flecks in his grey-green eyes. She thought to herself, "Jesse's alive and he has Caroline's eyes." She did not realize her gaze remained frozen on his face longer than necessary. Suddenly, they both diverted their eyes quickly back to his injured leg. A flush crossed her cheeks.

Jesse slowly peeled back a flap of fabric to reveal the slash from the bear's claws. "It's been many hours since he clawed you," Madison said with a concerned voice. " It looks deep. We should have looked after this right from the beginning. You had better let my mother disinfect and bandage it before you ride back home."

"You promised that I could just leave...no million questions to answer," Jesse argued. "I'll be fine."

"Do you want to lose a leg or what?" Madison snapped back, frustrated at his lack of attention to the wound. "This could wind up serious if you leave it unattended. Look at it! It's inflamed already."

Jesse heaved a sigh of defeat. "Okay, but that means you're going to have to tell them about the bear...and they'll not let you in the mountains alone again once they hear that story. Of course, that might be a good thing." Then he added half under his breath "...for both of us."

Madison's shoulders drooped in frustration. "Great! I'm already in trouble for lying about going to work in the bank this morning. I'll be grounded until I'm ninety if I mention the bear." Madison picked up her hat, emptied the water from it and then slapped the hat against her leg roughly to disperse any remaining droplets. She angrily plunked it on her head until it stopped at her ears. "You being alive...and now that dang bear have complicated my life something fierce."

Jesse's leg was throbbing badly, and his mood was slowly deteriorating. He grumbled back at her as he retrieved Redtip from the stream's edge. "Then you should have let the bear eat me. No one in your family believes I exist anyway. I'm a phantom, aren't I?" He swung up into his saddle, grimacing as he raised his injured leg over the seat. "Seeing as my leg is killing me, I'll let your mother look at it, but I'll not be put through a trial just because I happen to exist."

8

The couple rode slowly toward the farmyard, scattering a gaggle of tame geese in the path of the horses as they entered the yard. Mel and Loretta Graham had seen them approaching from a distance, and waited anxiously on the veranda for the pair to travel closer. Both Mel and Loretta's faces were grim with the knowledge that their daughter had lied to them again, but their hearts were eternally grateful to see her home unharmed.

Timothy and Troy had their horses saddled, ready to leave in search of Madison, but seeing her approach, they tied the horses to the corral, and mounted the veranda to stand beside the Grahams.

Madison and Jesse rode close to the base of the veranda. By the glum look on the faces before them, the young pair knew they were about to face a firing squad. Madison swallowed nervously. She thought it best to lead with an apology. "I'm sorry, but due to circumstances which might have put...some people in danger, I thought it necessary for you to meet Jesse in person." She turned sideways in her saddle and put out her hand to introduce the young man who sat silently on his horse beside her. "This is Jesse...Jesse, these are my parents, brother Timothy and his friend, Troy."

Jesse nodded but they did not nod any greeting back. They simply stared in shock at the young man on his restless, chestnut horse. Madison sucked in an awkward breath. "Jesse can't stay...but he has a bad cut on his leg and I really think his wound should be looked at before he returns home."

No one on the veranda said a word. They continued to stare at Jesse as if he were an alien from another planet. Jesse's horse fidgeted and danced a bit beside the calm Timber. "I'd better go," he whispered low to Madison." I'll be okay. I'll see you later." He turned Redtip away to leave.

"Over my dead body," stormed Troy, pushing his way to the front of the veranda. "You come near her again and I'll knock you clean off that ill-trained nag of yours." Timothy grabbed his friend quickly to hold him back, remembering that Jesse was the son of a former gunslinger and might have inherited his father's quick trigger-finger.

Mel and Loretta both stepped forward to calm Troy. Then Mel turned to his daughter.

"This lying and sneaking around, Maddy, has to come to an end. I don't care if this fellow is Jesse or not. It doesn't excuse you lying to your family. Do you realize how much it hurts us that we can't trust you anymore? Went to town and saw the bank closed. Near to made your mother sick with worry."

Madison bit her lip and tears filled her eyes to hear her father speak of such mistrust in her. She knew she was guilty, but at the same time, she could think of nothing else that she might have done to prevent her brother and Troy from getting shot by Andy Kaleb.

Jesse cut in angrily. "She was just trying to protect your bloody son and his friend from getting their heads shot off by my Pa...and trust me, you and I know father could do it with his eyes closed." He pointed his finger straight at Troy. "Maybe if you were man enough, you'd not let a lady take the blame for your doings." With that, Jesse whirled his horse about and galloped out of the yard in a flurry of dust.

Timothy's shoulders sagged as he stepped forward to face his father. "He spoke the truth, Father. Troy and I were planning to go up there tonight and see if this Jesse character was a ghost or not. Guess Madison must have heard us planning it and went to warn them not to shoot us." He called out to Madison sheepishly, "Sorry Sis."

Troy did not apologize. He was not yet finished with this Jesse Kaleb character.

Mel turned to his daughter, who still sat upon Timber at the base of the veranda. "Put Timber in the corral, and come discuss a few things. Perhaps you had a sound reason for lying, but we still can't have this kind of deception in the house. You should have come to us with the problem instead of endangering yourself going into the mountains."

"You boys get yourselves in here, as well," Loretta scolded, giving Timothy a swat on the pants as he entered the house. With the men out of earshot, Loretta turned to smile at Madison. "So Jesse's alive. Glory be! Don't know if he's a ghost or an angel, but he's sure a good looking one."

Madison broke into a wide smile of relief. "I never noticed," she lied, but the mutual smile between the women revealed the truth. Madison turned Timber towards the corral. As she pulled the saddle off of Timber, she worried about the wound on Jesse's leg. If she hadn't lied about going to work, perhaps she could have talked her parents into letting her bring them some antibiotics for his leg tomorrow. Telling a lie was like stretching an elastic band. Sooner or later, it always snapped back and slapped you in the face.

ଓଃ

The Graham family and Troy sat at the long kitchen table, and promised to practice more honesty in solving problems, Madison thought that this was a good time to voice her concern over Jesse's injury. In doing so, she was once again caught concealing a secret.

"How did he injure his leg?" her mother asked, and the question dropped Madison's soul to the floor. She could no longer lie to them, especially after their discussion on exercising better trust in the family.

"Well, he was attacked by a bear." She proceeded to tell them the whole story, and as she revealed the frightening experience, Loretta buried her face in her hands in realization of what could have easily happened to both Madison and Jesse Kaleb. She had always feared Madison riding alone in the mountains and now her fears were substantiated.

Mel's face turned white, while Timothy and Troy's eyes grew larger than duck eggs, their youthful minds centered on the excitement, and less oblivious to the danger.

"Were you ever going to tell us about this...if the boy hadn't been harmed?" her father asked suspiciously, his trust in her once again questioned.

Madison lowered her eyes and answered truthfully. "I was afraid you'd never let me ride in the mountains again if I told you about the bear attack."

Her father put both hands over his face and rubbed them up and down in frustration. He looked at her long and hard. At first he had thought the mystery of secret glens and waterfalls lured his daughter into the mountains, as it had done to himself and many others who loved the mountainous scenery. But now he had a feeling the boy had something to do with it, and this stranger was perhaps more dangerous than all the other perils of the mountain, because Mel Graham did not believe this young man was Jesse Kaleb.

"Strange," Mel puzzled aloud. "I remember young Jesse when he used to come with his father to get barley and oats. He'd broken his arm as a four year old, and ever since, he favored it and always held the reins in his right hand. Wonder why he switched to reining with his left hand?"

Troy's eyes widened, eager to grasp onto any questionable scenario about Jesse. "I don't trust him," he blurted out. "There's no way he could live in those mountains for the past dozen years and never be seen by anyone, or want to come down out of the mountains himself for some reason or other...and did you see the way he wore his gun, tied low like a gunfighter? Who taught him that? No one wears a gun like that 'les they're out gunning for somebody...or hiding in the mountains so's they don't get hanged. Likely holding the Kalebs captive...threatening them if they don't cooperate."

"Oh, for gracious sake, Troy," Madison cut in with frustration. "I'm sure he fixed the barn while holding them at gunpoint...Anyhow, it's their business."

"Only so long as it doesn't involve you. Then it's our business," her brother cut in. "They're a loony bunch. I don't like anything about that lot."

"Well, you sure seemed to like her biscuits and honey when we visited," Madison replied haughtily, and Timothy shook his head and exited, before he got into a fight with his sister. Troy followed him, well aware that Madison usually had the final say anyway.

Loretta had been fairly quiet through the conservation, and now suggested, "I still have some left-over disinfectant, salve and bandages that Dr. Fescue gave me when your father stepped on that nail a while back. Could be if you and your father left early in the morning, you might pay them a visit and give them this stuff for his leg. Sure hate to see gangrene set in just because we never made an effort to help the boy...and if the bear is dead, well, that's one less danger on the trail for you both to run into. Maybe if your Father saw things first-hand up there, we'd get a better understanding of the situation."

Mel nodded his head in agreement. "I need to get some honest answers from Andy, that's for sure. There's another thing that bothers me. Whose boy did they think they buried?"

9

Jesse left his horse saddled in the corral, and leaned weakly on one leg against the gate. He was nauseous and dizzy, and his leg felt on fire. "Sorry, Redtip. I'll unsaddle you later." He limped towards the house and struggled to mount the steps onto the veranda.

Andy knew instantly that something was wrong when he spied Jesse's chestnut left saddled in the corral. It was an unwritten law that one cares for your horse first, for your life often depended on the well being of your horse. Andy knew Jesse would never leave Redtip saddled without good reason. He quickened his pace to the house to see what the problem was. Andy caught up to Jesse just as the young man sat down on the top steps of the veranda to rest his injured leg.

Jesse was quickly hustled inside, and his injured leg cleansed carefully by Caroline. Having little medical supplies, Andy tipped a bottle of whiskey and poured it over the wound before the unsuspecting Jesse had time to prepare for the pain. Jesse sunk his fingernails deep into the mattress. "You could have warned me," he moaned painfully.

"It's alcohol. Best I can do to kill the infection tonight," Andy explained. "Can't take you down the mountain in a wagon in the dark. Too risky. Have to wait for dawn to get you to a doc. Then I'll hitch up Skat."

"It's cut deep. Should have stitches," Caroline informed both the men. "I think I better boil some thread and a needle."

"Don't you go making any of those fancy loop stitches like on your tablecloths," Jesse tried to jest, but he was feeling feverish and sick to his stomach, and at this moment, he didn't care what fancy stitch she put in his leg.

"It's going to hurt," Andy warned and Jesse nodded.

"Should have listened to Madison when she wanted to take care of it in the beginning," Jesse repented, and winced as he reached down to grab his thigh.

"Always listen to a lady," Andy advised. "Now you want to bite on something while she does her stitching, or do you want to drink the other half of this whiskey bottle?"

"Depends whether you made that brew yourself or not. Likely live longer without it."

"You're a smart man," Andy agreed and sat the bottle back on the table, but not before he took one sip for himself just to calm his nerves.

Caroline washed her hands carefully and pushed a fine disinfected thread through the head of a boiled needle. Jesse closed his eyes tight and clenched his teeth, ready for the oncoming stitching. Andy held Jesse's leg firm to the bed as Caroline nimbly pulled the wound together with skill and speed. "Had to stitch up a few horses in my time," she said to Jesse.

"Your hide's a whole lot easier to push the needle through. There! Done!" She rose and gathered bandages to cover the wound.

Jesse sunk his head back deep into a pillow. He took a few deep breaths to allow the pain to subside a bit. "Did the horses live?" he uttered, as Caroline carefully bandaged his leg.

"Two out of three," she replied with honesty and calmness, and patted his hand with a reassuring, motherly touch.

"That's a good average," Jesse murmured, and began to drift into slumber. He was exhausted from the day's event with the bear, and riding over six hours with an injured leg. "Redtip needs unsaddling," he remembered, as his head flopped sideways on the pillow. He was asleep before Andy could reassure him that his horse would be taken care of.

૪ૹ

Early the next morning, Jesse sat on the edge of his bed, feeling less feverish and more rested. His leg had throbbed all night, but he felt stronger. Andy still insisted that he take Jesse down to the doctor in Northfork, but Jesse was reluctant to leave the Kaleb farm. If anyone would be able to distinguish him from the real Jesse, it would be Dr. Fescue who had delivered Caroline's baby and who had taken care of the boy's body after drowning. Jesse insisted that he would be fine, but Andy did not want to take a chance on infection settling into his wound.

Mid morning, Mel Graham and his daughter arrived at the Kaleb farmyard. Mel was shocked at the improvement in the yard and buildings. The place had been sadly neglected on his last visit. Sudden change aroused suspicion in Mel Graham. If Jesse was alive, there would have been a gradual improvement on the homestead as the boy grew into manhood, so why the sudden change now?

Jesse sat on the edge of the bed, a blanket draped across his lap, revealing one leg of underwear rolled up above his wound. A handsome Jesse looked up at Madison as she entered the kitchen and approached him. Without his hat, she could not help but notice the tousle of fair curls on his head. The young man did not make eye contact with her father, as Jesse remembered his last words to Troy had been harsh.

Mel handed Caroline a sack of medical supplies, telling her that they had been left over from a previous wound to himself. Caroline accepted gratefully, and immediately unloaded the sack on the table to see what supplies she could use for Jesse's injury.

Madison sat on a chair adjacent to Jesse. "How's the leg this morning?"

"Better, I think. Mother stitched it up neat as a ripped sheet...but father near to killed me disinfecting it with his homemade whiskey. I hope your mother sent something a little more humane."

Madison laughed, her eyes sparkling with humor and relief to see Jesse in reasonable health. "Do you mean to drink or to put on the wound?"

Jesse laughed in return. "Both!" The exchange of laughter between the two young people did not go unnoticed by Mel Graham. A worried frown etched between his eyes.

Caroline approached Jesse, and kneeled down to carefully remove his bandages. He winced as she unwrapped the wound and displayed a gash the width of a man's hand upon his swollen leg.

"Perhaps you could advise me on the wound," Caroline asked of Mel. "Do you think Andy should take him down to see Dr. Fescue?"

Mel kneeled on one knee to take a closer look at Jesse's wound. "I don't like to make decisions concerning other people's health, but claw wounds from animals can be more infectious than a cut from a clean knife or axe...and it looks inflamed and swollen, so I'd have the doc take a look at it. Nice stitch job though. Doc will be impressed."

"Then that's settled," Andy declared. "Use them disinfectant things on his leg, Carrie, and I'll hitch Skat to the wagon. We'll want to arrive in Northfork before nightfall."

Jesse went to argue but Andy held one finger up to halt his words. "You're going."

Jesse closed his mouth, and respectfully obeyed the elder. He knew Andy and Caroline had lost one son, and Andy was taking no chance on losing another.

"Could you stay with Caroline until we get back, Madison?" Andy asked with a desperate plea. "I'll take you back down to the valley in the morning. Caroline gets scared alone after dark. Thinks she hears the puma about. I'd take her along, but it's a long rough ride in the wagon for her."

Madison agreed willingly, anxious to visit with Caroline. Mel was uncomfortable with the arrangement, but decided the worst Caroline could do was fill Madison's head with more stories.

Once at the bottom of the mountain, Mel cut off towards his homeplace, and Andy proceeded alone with Jesse into Northfork.

10

As evening fell on the Kaleb household, oil lamps and candles were lit to brighten the dark corners of the kitchen. Because Madison had shown such interest in Caroline's dishes, Caroline decided to open her large trunk and show Madison other treasures that she had collected throughout the years. Caroline handed Madison photos of her parents and her wedding, and held up fancy ribbons she had once worn in her hair to a special concert as a young lady. Madison's favorite discoveries became the flowers that Caroline had once pressed and kept crisp as linen between the pages of old books.

As Madison carefully turned the pages to reveal pressed violets and wild bluebells, a certificate tumbled from a book into her lap. Madison picked up the certificate and realized it was a birth certificate for a baby boy called Jesse, born in Boston four years before the Jesse that she knew had been born to the Kalebs in Northfork. Madison frowned. The birth certificate stated no father's name, only that of the mother, Caroline Alissa Randall. As Madison peered at the certificate, she realized Caroline must have borne a child before she married Andy Kaleb. She tried to slip the certificate back into the book without Caroline noticing, but it was too late.

Caroline snatched the birth certificate and for a few moments glared at Madison, as if she had intruded on a very private secret.

"I...I'm sorry," Madison stuttered awkwardly. "I...didn't mean to read it. It just fell from the book and..."

Caroline collected herself and took a deep breath. "It's okay, dear. I can see you now realize I had a child out of wedlock before I met Andy. I was sheltered a lot by my Aunt and Grandfather Lewis after my parent's death. My mother's father was a stern and powerful man, and scared off prospective suitors. Then one day, this stranger rode into town, handsome as they come. Baxter seemed to single me out. I realize now it was because he was trying to make a deal supplying horses to my grandfather's freight line. Grandfather Lewis never liked him. Said any man who went by only one name could never be traced or trusted. I wouldn't believe my grandfather's suspicions. I started slipping out at night to meet him, and that's where a child came into being. Grandfather Lewis was humiliated to discover me unwed and expecting a child." Caroline pushed to her feet and slowly closed the chest. "He didn't want anyone in the community to know about it. Kept me hidden until the child was born."

"Didn't the father take some responsibility?" Madison asked sadly.

"When I told Baxter I was with child, he disappeared fast as a slippery coyote, along with grandfather's money for thirty horses. Never found or heard from him again. Grandfather was angry as a hornet about the stolen money, and said he didn't want the man's child in his house." Caroline smoothed her hair back with a sad sigh. "Guess he got his wish. My child died shortly after birth. A year later, my Aunt met a man from Canada and they married and left, so I decided to leave Boston as well, and travel out west to make a new life. I met Andy on the train. He was a guard for the railroad company and wore a gun on his hip. Folks were scared stiff of him on the train, saying he used to be a gunfighter, but I witnessed Andy sneaking candies to the children on the train all the way to Northfork, so by the time the train arrived, I'd fallen in love with the man."

Caroline chuckled. "Poor grandfather gave up on me when he found out I'd married a former gunslinger. Disowned me. Figured I'd gone from one devil to another, but that wasn't so. Andy was a good man and I could see it from the start. Gave up his guns and we hit to farming. Came up here high in the mountains to escape fellows who were always wanting to test how fast he could draw a gun. Been a good man to me all our days, and a good father to our son."

"Does he know about the first child?" Caroline asked quietly, not knowing if she should pry further into such a sensitive situation.

"Yes. It was Andy who named our second son, Jesse, after my first child."

Caroline's eyes misted for a moment. Then suddenly, her face blossomed into sunshine, as if she had quickly closed one door and opened another. "Let's have a cup of tea and some biscuits, shall we? I'll even wrap some up for you to take back for your brother."

଄ઙ

Jesse bounced along in the wagon, trying as best as he could to support his leg so the roughness of the ride wouldn't break open the stitches and cause bleeding to start again. He turned to Andy and confessed, "I've been remembering a lot of my past these last few months."

"Good! Good!", Andy said, but at the same time, his face saddened, as the more Jesse's past revealed itself, the farther he feared it may eventually take Jesse away from him and Caroline.

"I'm remembering more about my Aunt Krystaline. She used to send me down the street to a woodworker. I guess she knew I missed working with Guilbert in the wood shop. I was about thirteen or so by that time, and Sol Barns would have me sweep floors and pick up scraps of wood in exchange for taking the scraps home to Aunt Krystaline for kindling. After she got sick and died, he let me stay on. Gave me a cot in the back room, and fed me in payment for cleaning the place up everyday. Made me go to school too...said he promised my Aunt before she died. Later, I started working beside him as a fellow carpenter, and did so for many years. Likely learned more about wood working from Sol than Guilbert."

Jesse shifted his weight on the hard wagon-seat. "Then one day, some runaway team of horses mowed him down in the streets...and he was gone...and my future was gone...like someone blew out a candle."

Jesse sighed in memory of the kind woodworker who had taken him in. "He didn't have any wife or kids or relatives in this country. He said he got into a bit of trouble in England and his parents shipped him abroad at fifteen. He never saw them again. Anyhow, after he got run over, his relatives from overseas sold all his assets through a lawyer...and that was that. Sort of like Sol Barns plain evaporated...except for the fine furniture he left behind." He gave a short laugh. "I kind of like to think his furniture will outlast all those relatives of his that never gave a hoot about him when he was alive."

Jesse changed positions on the wagon seat again, trying to find an impossible seat of comfort that would not bother his throbbing leg. "After Sol died, the banker gave me a letter that he had kept in safe keeping for me. I reckon Aunt Krystaline had given it to Sol before she died. All it said was, "Guilbert said you ran away from Birchman's Orphanage. Go there and ask about a man called Sterling."

Andy's forehead wrinkled. "That's a strange note. Did you ask about it at the orphanage?"

"Yes, but when I told them about the note and asked who Sterling was, the Head Mistress ushered me quickly out the door and said, "Don't stir up skeletons." She wouldn't tell me a thing...so I went from door to door in the neighborhood. Finally found one lady who once worked at the orphanage who knew something about a man with that name."

Jesse reached over and took the reins out of Andy's hands, and pulled Skat to a stop. "Skat needs a rest and my leg needs a break...It turns out this elderly woman was once a cleaner at the orphanage. In later years, she worked for Krystaline and told my aunt about an old gentleman arriving one night with a newborn baby boy. Gossip between workers at the orphanage was that a man called Sterling paid the orphanage a great deal of money for them to keep quiet about who brought the child there."

"Did you ever find out who this Sterling fellow was?" Andy questioned.

Jesse shook his head. "No, but Krystaline must have thought I was that baby. Otherwise, why would she even mention it to me. I figured Sterling was likely dead by now, so checked cemetery markers and obituaries, but found no Sterling. The cleaning lady said Sterling came only twice to the orphanage to donate money. After that, he said the problem had gone out west and he was rid of it."

Jesse slapped the reins upon Skat's back to signal the horse to move out again, and then handed the reins back to Andy. "I gave up the search. Figured I was blessed with good parents along the way like Guilbert Rideau, Aunt Krystaline and Sol Barns, and now you and Caroline. A man can't ask for more than that."

Andy nodded in agreement, "Blood is just history, son. It doesn't make you a parent. Only love can do that. I'm glad you had a few good, caring folk in your life. They made you into a good man."

Jesse accepted the compliment with a gentle smile. "After Sol's death, I decided to travel back to Riverflats. I don't know what I expected to find there. Surely no welcome from Harry, but I wanted to pay my respects to Guilbert again, and guess it was just a direction to point my nose at...roots of some sort, I suppose. That's why I ended up in the mountains, passing this way when the storm hit, trying to take a short cut to Riverflats."

"Glad you can finally piece these things together. It'll put your mind to rest some," Andy said. "You know, you're always welcome to stay with us, but I'll understand if you want to get back to civilization where a young man should be."

"Kind of had enough of civilization for awhile."

Andy nodded in agreement. '"Yeah, those quiet mountain peaks sorta tip the scale in their favor, don't they."

The doctor listened quietly as Andy simply explained the young man had been clawed by a bear. The doctor looked at the wound and commented on Caroline's good stitching job. He examined and disinfected the wound, bandaged it once again, and handed some bottles of disinfectant to Andy. Andy took some coins out of his jacket to pay for the appointment and medicine while Jesse rolled his pant leg back down.

"Looks like you've had a good nurse," the doctor said to Jesse. "Come back and I'll take the stitches out in two weeks time, and check on the wound. If it gets worse, get back here. Keep listening to Caroline and you'll save your leg. Get sloppy at treating it before it's healed and you'll lose it. You hear me."

"Yes sir," Jesse replied.

"Now I need your name for my records. You are...?"

Jesse glanced at Andy, hesitating a moment to allow Andy time to confide in the doctor. When Andy said nothing, Jesse replied calmly, "Jesse Kaleb."

Dr. Fescue lowered his glasses and slowly turned to look at Jesse. The doctor reached out and took Jesse's left arm, feeling the bones in the elbow of the young man. "You're not the same Jesse I set with a broken arm near twenty years ago."

"Never said I was," Jesse replied. "You just asked my name and I said it was Jesse Kaleb. Thank you for your care. I appreciate it." Jesse picked up his hat and exited the room. The doctor looked anxiously at Andy, but Andy only uttered a word of thanks to the doctor and hurried to catch up to Jesse, who was outside and climbing hastily into the wagon.

As they left Northfork, Jesse burst into concern. "I think we're getting in too deep with my identity. I know we want to protect Caroline, but I don't know if me pretending I'm Jesse is going to work for much longer. The doctor knows I'm not your son. He's likely going to the sheriff as we speak, thinking I'm taking advantage of you and Caroline in some way."

"I thought Caroline and I weren't hurting anyone," Andy expressed sadly, his eyes drifting off across the valley towards the protection of the mountains. "Guess as long as we stayed up in the mountains, it seemed okay to let Carrie pretend, so long as she was happy. Now we've put you in an awkward situation...forced you to lie to the doc...and to Madison...and you know Mel's daughter is going to shoot you full of lead when she finds out you mislead her."

Jesse removed his hat and ran his fingers through sandy, curly hair. He let his breath out with a long whistle. "Yeah! Ma keeps reminding me Madison can shoot a pea out of a pod at fifty feet. I'm going to be dead, aren't I...dead as a bug on a wheel." Both men burst into laughter and hurried Scat into a faster trot.

⁂

It was past midnight when their wagon rolled into the Kaleb homestead. A lantern was glowing from the front veranda, and sent a guiding beam to the house. They quietly entered the cabin, figuring Caroline and Madison to be asleep in the master bedroom, as no lamp had been left burning on the table. Andy lit the lamp and carried it with him towards the cot by the wall, thinking he and Jesse would be bedding there for the night.

Jesse limped over and discovered Madison sound asleep in the cot. He stared down at her, and complained to Andy. "First, she takes my horse. Now she takes my bed."

Andy was somewhat surprised. "Thought the ladies would bunk down together in our bed, but looks like you've been demoted to the floor. I'll get you some blankets."

"No way. I've bounced in that wagon for half a day. I'm sleeping in my bed." Jesse sat down on the edge of his bed and removed his boots. He pulled his shirttails out of his jeans for comfort, and let his shirt fall open. Then he turned and slowly pushed Madison over a foot or two. Madison moaned, but did not waken. He lay down on his back and then abruptly sat up again. He turned towards Madison and gradually slid his pillow out from beneath her head. He fluffed the feather pillow up and lay it beneath his own head. "My bed. My pillow."

Andy had been standing beside the bed, watching the whole episode with amusement. Now he just shook his head and whispered, "I've seen men shot for a whole lot less, son. Yes, I surely have."

Andy retired to his bedroom, leaving Jesse to fight with Madison over bed space and blankets.

Madison turned over in the bed and her arm fell across Jesse's chest. He looked down at her hand resting warmly upon him. Gingerly, he lifted her hand up to lay it back beside her own body, but then changed his mind. Her hand felt rather nice upon his chest. He returned her arm where she had put it, smiled to himself and drifted off to sleep.

Madison woke earlier than Jesse, and was shocked to see him lying next to her. As she was on the far side of the bed next to the wall, there was no escaping the bed without climbing over Jesse. She deliberated on how she was going to do this without waking him. No one else was awake, so she maneuvered as close to his side as she could get, then tried to swing her leg over him to touch the floor on the other side. Such was not her luck! Both of his arms came up and encircled her back, holding her on top of him in a tight vice. She struggled but could not get free of his strong arms.

"Aaah!" he exclaimed, "And what little mouse have I caught in my bed?"

"Let go of me!" she demanded, her breathing deepened from their closeness. "I...I was waiting for you both to come home, and didn't mean to fall asleep on your bed. I was going to sleep with Caroline."

"Seems like a weak story to me."

Madison flung herself off of him and straightened her blouse and hair. Just then, Caroline came out of the bedroom and saw the ruffled Madison looking very upset.

"Oh my dear!. Andy should have woken us and made different arrangements. You had better have been a gentleman, Jesse, or I'll take the fly swatter to you." Then she turned to the stove to begin making breakfast, fully confident that her son had behaved respectfully.

Jesse tucked his shirttails into his pants, pulled on his boots and grabbed his hat. Andy insisted he stay indoors and rest his leg, but Jesse was anxious to escape Madison's fiery eyes, so he quickly limped out the door to do whatever chores he was capable of handling on one leg.

Andy immediately went to the woodpile and came back with a Y-necked branch for Jesse to use as a crutch.

The aroma of bacon and eggs coaxed the two men in early from chores. Andy shut the kitchen door behind him and informed Madison, "Jesse is out on the veranda and wants to speak to you for a few moments."

"With an apology, I suspect," Madison declared, wiping her hands on her apron. “He near to scared me half to death when I woke up this morning." Madison slipped out the kitchen door and closed it behind her.

Jesse was sitting on the railing and she could not help but think how handsome he looked with his sandy hair curling out from beneath the brim of his hat and his grey-green eyes blending in with the green background of pine. She approached him with an upward tilt to her chin. It was hard to appear mad at such a handsome young man.

Jesse in return, couldn't help but think how beautiful Madison looked with her hair unsuccessfully pulled up on top of her head, allowing a fall of unruly curls to fall on her shoulders and bounce against her cheeks.

"Can I trust you to keep a secret?" he asked, his face suddenly serious and eyes looking away, as if he did not want to make eye contact with her.

"Depends," she replied warily, not trusting his serious air all of a sudden.

"You know Caroline has clung to the belief that Jesse never died and has fantasized him to be alive all these years."

Madison's eyes squinted and a huge frown wrinkled her forehead, "But they weren't fantasies. You're real."

Suddenly the kitchen door burst open and Caroline called to them. "Breakfast will get cold. Come in. You can apologize to her later."

Jesse's mouth dropped open in dismay as he followed the ladies in from outdoors. "Apologize for what?" He limped to the table, complaining further. "First she takes my horse. Now she takes my bed, and I have to apologize." He plunked himself down at the table adjacent from her and moved the platter of bacon closer to himself. "Likely going to eat half my bacon too."

Caroline slapped his fingers with a spatula. "Time for grace...and just remember who brought you the bacon in the first place."

With breakfast over, Andy saddled Timber and Scat and brought the horses to the house, ready to accompany Madison safely back down the mountain. Caroline thanked Madison for caring for her while the men were gone, and they hugged goodbye, knowing it would likely be a lengthy time before they would see each other again.

Jesse leaned against the open door frame to the kitchen, relaxing his sore leg and watching the women embrace. Madison finally said her last goodbyes and began dismounting the veranda steps. Part way down, she paused and turned to look up at Jesse. "Take care of your leg."

He smiled mischievously back at her. "Take care of my horse."

Madison wrinkled her nose at his teasing, and turned to continue down the steps. At the bottom step, she paused again, spun around and ran up the steps in a flurry. She threw her arms around Jesse's neck and planted a deep, passionate kiss on his lips. Then she turned and ran down the steps. At the bottom, she turned around again and yelled, "I just wanted to make sure you were real." Then she mounted her horse and quickly rode out of the yard.

Jesse stood in shock, unmoving and not uttering a word. He simply stared as Andy and Madison disappeared behind the pines. The girl had completely caught him off guard. He put his fingers to his lips, which were still feeling the sensation of Madison's passionate kiss.

"I think that girl is going to get me into a whole mess of trouble down in the valley," he muttered to Caroline.

Caroline just smiled as she rinsed the china teapot and placed it carefully back in the china cabinet.

Jesse flung himself down on his cot to rest his throbbing leg, mumbling, "She don't need to think a little kiss like that is going to let her take everything I own."

11

Troy restrained his thoughts and feelings about Jesse Kaleb to the Graham family, but inwardly, his jealousy grew stronger daily, knowing that Madison was increasingly fascinated by the stranger. He wanted to prove to her that Jesse was potentially a dangerous imposter. He knew there was nothing he could say that would change Madison's mind, so he had to either make Jesse confess or find some way to reveal his true identity.

Troy highly doubted that Timothy would take part in any more plans to visit the Kalebs, so he had to do something by himself. If Madison could see Jesse for the phony that he was, then maybe she would see himself more favorably in comparison.

Troy Bennett travelled to Northfork, hitting first to Dr. Fescue's office, for he believed the doctor to be the most knowledgeable man on the deceased Jesse Kaleb. Having known Troy all his life, Dr. Fescue sympathized with Troy's concern for Madison and the Kalebs. He also could not understand why this stranger had taken on the identity of Jesse Kaleb, whom he had declared dead himself many years before.

"As a doctor, I can't reveal anyone's health problems," Dr. Fescue informed Troy, "You realize that is a private matter. But I can tell you one thing...I was never visited by Jesse Kaleb yesterday. That's all I'll say on the matter."

That was enough for Troy and he could not scoot across the street and into the sheriff's office fast enough. Sheriff Bailey shrugged his shoulders. "Doc told me the same thing, but I can't do anything until a crime is committed. It's no crime to call yourself Jim, Jack or Joe. Got no posters up on him. Doc said the two looked chummy enough, so didn't look like Andy was in any kind of danger...and Andy wore his gun, so that's all I need to know. If Andy's got his gun, he'll take care of himself."

Troy left the sheriff's office disheartened. Who else could he turn to? He sat on his horse at the gateway to town, and his eyes drifted to the sign pointing to Riverflats. The sun was still high in the sky and he figured he had time to scout out the neighboring town before returning home. Maybe he'd find the woodworker who would testify he'd made Caroline's cabinet and Madison's engraved chest, and then he could prove to Madison that the whole Jesse Kaleb affair was a farce.

Troy first visited the sheriff's office in Riverflats, describing Jesse and Andy's appearance, and asking if the sheriff had seen them. The sheriff was wary to answer, seeing as he had always liked Gil Rideau and wanted no harm coming to him. He was not sure of Troy's reason for wanting to know about the two men. "They was here a short while back," the sheriff cautiously revealed to Troy, "looking for a relative. Don't know where they've gone now. What's your stake in it?"

Excitement boiled in Troy's veins at the thought of a relative who could maybe spill more light on the situation. "We're friends. Been trying to help them find the same relative. Any chance they found...the person?"

The sheriff eyed the young man in front of him. He looked clean-cut enough; hair cut, shaved, clean shirt, good quality horse tied outside to the hitching post, no gun on his hip, just a rifle slid in a scabbard on the saddle. The sheriff took all these things in with a keen eye for troublemakers. He decided he could trust Troy.

"Down by the river. Old fellow in a shack...scruffy, usually drunk, nasty tongue. Keep ten paces back or he'll spit in your eye."

Troy gave a quick thanks and aimed for the shack by the river. He wasn't able to ask the sheriff whose relative the old man was without looking suspicious, so now he could only hope the relative belonged to Jesse, not Andy or Caroline. If the relative belonged to Jesse, then maybe he could bring him back to the Grahams and have him reveal who Jesse really was. He was delighted that his plan was turning out so positive.

Troy dismounted his horse outside the shack. A curl of smoke twisted from a crooked chimney pipe, so he figured someone must be inside. A thin donkey lifted his head, and then continued to graze amongst the tall weeds, which had taken over much of the area surrounding the shack. Troy knocked on the door and heard no reply. He took hold of the handle to open the door when the door was pulled open with one mighty yank from inside, sending Troy flying into the chest of a burly, unshaven man who reeked of whiskey.

Troy collected himself and stood erect, straightening his hat. He stepped back a few paces, remembering the sheriff's warning about the spitting. "I hear you are a relative of...a friend of mine...young man, blondish curly hair, rides a chestnut."

Harry's eyes narrowed into two catlike slivers. "Friend, you say. Well now, ain't that nice that you paid me a visit. Did my nephew send some whiskey for his dear old uncle?"

Troy fidgeted and shoved his hands in his pockets so the man wouldn't see them shaking. "No...well...he doesn't talk much. Hard to get a word out of him. Uncle, you say? Are you his only relative?"

Harry's arm snapped out quick as a snake, and his big hand grasped Troy's shirt, twisting the collar until Troy gasped for breath. Troy could not free himself from Harry's powerful hold on his throat, and feared for his life. Harry's voice boomed like thunder. "Well, if I can't get him hung, then maybe I'll just get his friend hung instead. Tired of waiting for the thief to come back."

Harry had Troy's collar twisted up to his throat in such a tight vise that Troy's voice came out in a squeak. "H-Hung for what?"

"Well now, let's see," Harry said almost playfully, a wicked smile advertising stained teeth from chewing tobacco daily. "The plan was I kill my brother. Gil kills me in revenge. Gil hangs...But, seeing as you're here instead, how about I kill my brother. You kill me. You hang."

Troy swallowed painfully. "I...I don't like that plan very much...and to tell the truth, I...I don't like your nephew very much either. He's..."

Harry laughed loudly and flung the young man across the room like a feather cushion. Troy smashed across the table, flipping it upside down, and crumbling to the floor amongst broken table legs. Harry slid a revolver across the floor to Troy, and then slowly pulled a gun from his gun belt. With a smirk upon his lips, he aimed the revolver at Troy and cocked the trigger.

Troy put his arm up to cover his face. "I've got no quarrel with you, Mister. I barely know your nephew. In fact, I..." - BOOM! A bullet hit Troy in the leg and he yelped and grasped his thigh in shock.

"Are you crazy?" Troy yelled in horror. BOOM! Another bullet entered his shoulder and thrust him back flat on the floor in pain.

Troy struggled to a sitting position, gripping his shoulder in agony. Blood spilled between his fingers. "What in hell are you doing?" BOOM! A third bullet clipped the top of his ear and splintered the table behind Troy's head. Troy felt wet, warm blood running down the side of his face and neck, and saw the revolver at his side. He heard the big man cock his gun again, and without looking up, Troy grabbed the revolver with his bloody hand and shot in the direction of the man.

Harry looked down at the fresh bullet hole in his chest, dropped the revolver and looked at Troy with a triumphant look on his face. "Been waiting." Then Harry collapsed like a mighty wall of thunder.

Troy looked down at his smoking gun and dropped it, kicking it away from himself with distaste. He had never intended to take another person's life, not ever in his lifetime unless he had to defend his country or family. All he wanted to be was a peaceful farmer, just a peaceful, soil-tilling farmer whose biggest concern was the weather and the markets.

Suddenly, people burst into the cabin like a swarm of bees. Having heard the shots from a distance away, they feared Harry was on another drunken rage. They checked

Harry's body, and then came to offer Troy assistance with his wounds. The sheriff entered shortly afterwards. He took a quick, observant look around the room, stepped over Harry, and kneeled beside Troy who was trying to rise to his feet. "Help is coming. Lay still or you'll bleed to death."

Several people kneeled beside Troy, attempting to stop the bleeding. "He kept shooting me," Troy panted between painful gasps of air, "telling me he was going to make me hang for something his nephew did. I don't know what. He just kept shooting. I had to shoot back. I swear it was in self defense."

The sheriff patted him on the shoulder. "Don't worry, kid. I believe you. Bad blood between Harry and his nephew. You got in the middle of it. I should have warned you."

Troy was angry at being caught in Jesse's web, and couldn't wait to disclose him as a phony to Madison. "The big man said something about killing his brother so his nephew would kill him and then hang for it...Then he decided to substitute me for his nephew. What kind of a crazy bunch are they?"

Sheriff Fillion's mouth dropped in surprise. "So Harry is the one who killed Guilbert. Always wondered who done such a cowardly deed. Clubbed his own brother. Well, Guilbert certainly deserved better than that." He turned to several men who were standing, waiting for the doctor to arrive. "Might as well load Harry in the wagon. You can bury him up yonder on the hill beside his brother. If there's any forgiveness coming to the man, it'll come from Guilbert...certainly not from me or this town."

ଔ

A deputy from Riverflats rode to Northfork to inform Sheriff Bailey about what had happened to Troy Bennett. Sheriff Bailey instantly took off for the Bennett farm to notify the family of Troy's shoot-out with Harry, knowing that they would be wondering why their son had not returned home. Afternoon slipped into early dusk by the time he arrived to inform the Bennetts about Harry and Troy's encounter.

Troy's parents instantly hitched their team to a wagon and hit for Riverflats. On the way, they stopped by the Graham farmstead. Mel and Loretta noticed their wagon approaching quickly, and as the Bennetts were not known for pushing their horses at such a fast pace, they instantly feared someone was hurt or very ill. Likewise, Madison and Timothy hurried from the barnyard when they recognized the sheriff accompanying Troy's parents.

Sheriff Bailey explained the situation quickly, and then Troy's father turned to Madison. "I'm sorry, honey. Troy said you trusted that fella, but seems he's got a shady past, and our Troy near to killed over it."

Madison swallowed tears in her throat. She had honestly begun to believe Jesse Kaleb was who he pretended to be. "How...how is Troy? Will he be okay?" Never in the world would she want any harm to come to the neighbor's son. She felt devastated and guilty that she had introduced Jesse into all their lives.

Troy's parents shook their heads to indicate they did not know Troy's condition. Then they turned their horses about to hit towards Riverflats.

"I'm coming with you," Madison shouted, wiping her arm quickly across her cheek to erase an escaped tear. "You go ahead and I'll catch up on Timber."

Madison ran to the corral to saddle up Timber. Tears were dampening the front of her shirt as she quickly tightened the cinch on Timber's saddle. Timothy caught up to his sister, spun her around to face him, and then wrapped two brotherly arms about her in a sympathetic hug. He didn't say anything. Now was not the time to scold or take pride in being right about Jesse Kaleb.

Timothy tossed a saddle quickly on his own horse. Madison understood his need to come with her to see Troy. Troy was Timothy's best friend, and the closest thing to a brother.

As they left the yard, their father handed a fistful of money up to Timothy. "It's late. Be nightfall when you get there. Get a hotel room. Tell Troy's father, I'll slip over and do his chores while he's gone, so not to hurry home. When you get back, we'll deal with Jesse." Timothy nodded and hurried after Madison and the others at a swift gallop.

CS80

"I got nothing to go after Gil for," Sheriff Fillion of Riverflat tried to explain to the Bennett and Graham families, and to Sheriff Bailey from Northfork. The Riverflat sheriff stood firm beside Troy's bedside and tried to make them understand. "Gil was an adopted lad by Guilbert Rideau. After Guilbert died, he was sent back east to an aunt in Boston. He'd be about thirteen years old at that time. He's had nothing to do with his uncle here ever since, so what his uncle did today puts no blame on Gil.

Harry was jealous over Gil inheriting Guilbert's share of the carpenter business, which was considerably more than Harry's share. With the boy gone, Harry drank the rest of the business away. Gil came here to see him a week or so ago...first time since he was a kid. Then went on his way back to where he come from with the other fellow. If Gil took on another name, no crime in that. Maybe he did it to hide from Harry all these years...'cause Harry was always one nasty sucker to the kid."

"So you're telling me the only thing I can do is suck it up and not hold Jesse...Gil...or whoever he is ... accountable for two bullets in me that were meant for him, and a third bullet ripping the tip of my ear off, and me having to kill a man? What's the justice in that?" Troy complained bitterly.

Seeing Troy upset, the doctor ordered the visitors to take their business out of the hospital room and away from the patient, but Sheriff Fillion turned in the doorway and glanced back at Troy. "Too bad you got hurt, lad, but sometimes when folks snoop into business that ain't their own, well, they autta know there's always a chance they'll get bit by a snake."

"Now you're blaming me?" Troy yelled back, and the doctor once again tried to usher the sheriff out of the patient's room before Troy started to bleed again. Troy lowered his gaze to the foot of his bed. Not being able to blame Jesse Kaleb for causing him to have to kill a man, or for the painful injuries he was suffering, left Troy feeling like he was suffering for absolutely no reason at all.

The sheriff eyed the dejected young man lying with a bound leg and shoulder, and a head wrap about his ear. "Look on the bright side. You're alive to tell your children a terrific tale someday about how you got all those bullet scars." He turned on his heel and quietly closed the door behind him, much to the doctor's relief.

Troy shrugged and gave a resigned sigh. "Should have seen the warning signs when the sheriff told me to stand ten paces back."

Just then, the door reopened and the doctor stuck his nose in the door. There's a pretty young lady here to see you. Sable McKauw. Says she *thinks* she's still your friend. You feel like more company?"

Troy had not seen Sable for some time, seeing as he had tried to patch up his relationship with Madison, but the truth was, Sable had caught his eye and he might as well admit it. He nodded to the doctor to let her come in.

The doctor smiled back, "I thought so."

12

With supper dishes done, Andy, Caroline and Jesse gathered on the veranda to watch the sinking sun cast a red sky behind the silhouette of pine. Caroline withdrew two pieces of paper from her apron pocket and held them lovingly in her hands. "Where'd we put the boy?" she suddenly asked, and the question spread shock across Andy's face, for Caroline had never mentioned the boy before.

Andy withdrew his pipe slowly and gave a slight cough. "The boy?" he questioned, making sure he had not misunderstood her.

Caroline rocked a little faster in her rocking chair on the veranda. "The boy they found drowned in the river. Did we make him a nice sign?"

Andy swallowed and the glint of a tear wet his eyes. "A small cross. Laid him up by Copper Ridge. Scenery nice there."

Caroline's gentle voice was almost lost in the creaking of her rocking chair. "We should get Jesse to make a real nice sign for him, seeing as he has a way with carving wood. Would you do that for us, Jesse?"

Jesse rose from where he sat on the veranda steps, and kneeled in front of her. "I would be honored to do that." He took her hands in his, and then noticed the two pieces of papers that she was holding.

"Two birth certificates," she informed him, and held them up towards the heavens. "Two sons taken from me...but God is gracious and gave me a third." She patted Jesse lovingly on the shoulder, as he kneeled before her. "You are not my Jesse Anthony. I realize that now. I have watched you work with your arm in ways that his injured arm could never have done...but never you mind. Where is it written in the laws that a mother can't have three Jesses?"

Jesse smiled. "It's a good name," and Caroline nodded in agreement. Jesse did not know she had birthed two sons. He was unsure if she was fantasizing again, and turned to Andy for validation of her statement. “Three Jesses?" he questioned Andy.

"She had another son before we met," Andy explained. "The child died shortly after birth. We named our second son after him."

Jesse nodded sadly. “I'm so sorry for you both. What do you wish me to carve on the marker for the boy?"

Caroline peered down at the two birth certificates as if they were delicate china. On this marker, put "Jesse Anthony Kaleb". May he forgive me for not praying over his precious soul or bringing flowers to his grave, and doing all the things a good mother should have done...I just didn't want him to be gone."

Andy rose and put his arm about her shoulders. "There is nothing to forgive, Carrie. Every time you sat a plate at the table for him, you brought him flowers, and every time you lit a candle and sat it in the window to guide him home from the woodlot, you prayed for him."

Caroline wiped tears from her face with the corner of her apron. "Someday I would like to return to Boston, and find another wee grave, and we will put a nice marker there for him too. Sterling Lewis doesn't have a say in what I can put on my child's grave anymore."

"S...Sterling?" the words sputtered out of Jesse's lips like a stutter. Andy's mouth dropped open as he had never heard Caroline mention her grandfather's first name before. She had always referred to him simply as Grandfather Lewis.

Caroline touched her hand tenderly to Jesse's cheek. "Yes, Sterling Lewis was my mother's father. I lived with Grandfather Lewis and my Aunt after my parents were killed. Randall was my maiden name." She sighed sadly to remember the sad occasion of her child's short life.

"I was an unwed mother," she confessed to Jesse. "The father of the child disappeared, along with a lot of money that he owed my grandfather for horses." She pressed the birth certificate to her lips and gave the paper a kiss. "Poor wee innocent fellow. He died the next day." Caroline inhaled deeply and straightened her shoulders bravely. "Enough said! Time for the living. There will be time enough for those gone before when we join them in glorious heaven."

Jesse's face was white as a ghost as he gingerly picked up the birth certificates from her lap and looked at them carefully. He turned slowly to Andy. "The year of birth is the same year that a baby was brought to the orphanage by a man called Sterling."

He turned to Caroline, and swallowed several times before the words came out. "Is there anything about your first baby that might distinguish him from another...a birthmark maybe, anything you can remember?"

She shook her head." I only held him for such a short time. He had fair hair...like mine used to be...and he was beautiful."

Jesse put both hands on her shoulders and looked deep into her teary eyes. "I was left at the same orphanage in Boston as a newborn around that same date. My Aunt Krystaline told me to ask the orphanage about a man called Sterling who left a baby boy at the orphanage. Could it be that your child did not die at all, and that your Grandfather gave him to the orphanage?"

Caroline put her hand to her mouth in disbelief and shock. She rose to her feet, and tears spilled over her fingertips. "Oh, he wouldn't do that to me...and to his own great-grandson," she sobbed. "Oh, Grandfather just wouldn't." A pitiful moan escaped from the depth of her soul.

Jesse wrapped his arms about her, a sob escaping from his throat as he pressed her face to his chest.

Andy slowly pried the birth certificates from Jesse's fingers and read the dates to confirm what Jesse had told him. Then he looked at Jesse and Caroline and shook his head in astonishment. "Ironic!...Sterling Lewis did not want to give you his name, but it is his name that has traced you back to your mother. I'd say justice is finally served."

Caroline's grey-green eyes looked up into Jesse's, which were droplets taken from the same pool. She reached up and touched the blond curls which curled out from beneath his hat, so much like her own as a young girl.

"He said he buried the child to spare me the pain, and showed me the fresh plot. I believed him. He put a simple cross and bid me not to shame him further by putting our name on it, so I only put "Jesse, my Lamb" ...but...there must be no child buried there. Oh Jesse, he stole so many years from us...You should have known your brother."

Jesse could barely speak. "My brother is here," Jesse said and placed his hand over his heart. "I think his spirit must have guided me here."

ᴄᴓᴙᴐ

At first, Madison was not going to accompany her father and brother, and Sheriff Bailey to the Kaleb farmstead. She was angry and felt humiliated that Jesse had allowed her to believe he was Jesse Kaleb. However, she feared Caroline might be upset by any contradiction to her fantasy, so she convinced the men to speak privately to Jessie and Andy while she kept Caroline busy elsewhere.

Madison said absolutely nothing on the journey up into the mountains. She kept going over and over in her head on what she should say to Caroline. Caroline would be the one hurt in all of this. It was obvious that Jesse could no longer continue his masquerade as her son. Madison's temper increased as she rode along in silence.

Hours passed and finally the group of four wound their way through the pines and cliffs and into the Kaleb homestead. Sheriff Bailey's eyes circled the farmyard in amazement. "Somehow, I didn't expect to find the place in such good condition," he said to Mel. "Andy was good with a gun, but never with a hammer."

Andy and Jesse glanced up from within the corral when they saw the group approaching. Andy noted that Sheriff Bailey was one of the riders, along with Mel Graham who sat much too rigid in his saddle for the visit to be a neighborly one. Madison and Timothy trailed timidly behind, looking as if they did not want to be included in any part of the visiting party. Andy felt an old impulse to reach for his rifle, but he did not.

"Gil Rideau?" Sheriff Bailey belted out, but Jesse did not acknowledge the name.

"Came to inform you your Uncle Harry is dead," the sheriff yelled to Jesse. Andy and Jesse closed the corral gate behind them and approached the riders. The sheriff waited for them to walk closer, his eyes drinking in every movement Jesse made.

"Seems Troy Bennett approached your Uncle Harry and near got shot to death," the sheriff informed Jesse. "Shot 3 times until he shot back and killed Harry in self defense. Seems Harry got tired of waiting for your return, so decided to exchange your hide for Troy's." He looked straight at Jesse with an accusing eye. "The lad is lucky to be alive."

"What the hell was Troy doing at Harry's?" Jesse expressed angrily, mad that Troy had snooped into his private affairs. “Is he going to be okay?"

"Figure so." The sheriff leaned forward, and rested his arms across the saddle horn. "No thanks to you and your Uncle Harry. Now I come up here to let you know the score, and I've also got to tell you that whatever you got going on up here is causing folks to get concerned down in the valley. Troy went to get some answers and wound up near killed over it. Don't blame the kid for being concerned over folks that are like family to him. There's a lot of folk concerned for the safety of their young-uns and these decent folks up here."

Jesse went to speak, but Andy moved in front of him. "Don't see as our boy has harmed any of your youngsters that I know of." Andy looked straight at Madison. "Has my boy been disrespectful to you, girl? If he has, I'll whip him. Surely I will."

Madison shook her head, her cheeks flushing with embarrassment. Andy then turned to Timothy. "He been in your face over anything?" Timothy nervously shook his head, and lowered his chin so he would not make eye contact with Andy.

Andy then turned to the sheriff. "Seems like we got no problem here that I can tell."

The sheriff sighed and turned his attention to Jesse. "Okay then. It appears you inherited a shack and a bit of land and a donkey out of it all. Sheriff Fillion in Riverflats would be most obliging if you told him what to do with it."

"Give the shack and land to the church," Jesse replied. "I don't want a penny of it...but I'll take the donkey for mother. Harry owes me that much for the beatings he gave me."

Caroline approached the group swiftly, wiping flour from her hands on a fresh apron. Everyone had forgotten about Caroline. "Did you say a donkey? Oh, we could surely use one in with the goats to keep the wolves away...Now would all of you like to stay for tea...and pie. Made a fresh strawberry rhubarb pie."

The sheriff shook his head. "Nothing I would like better, Caroline, but I can't leave Northfork for much longer. It'll be evening by the time I get back...and if those Averly brothers know I'm gone, they'll will be racing their dang horses right down the main street and into the coffee shop again."

Timothy shifted his weight onto one foot in the stirrup for dismounting his horse, but his father spoke sharply. "We got chores, Tim." The young man's face fell as he visioned the taste of strawberry rhubarb pie, and he settled back in the saddle grudgingly.

"I'll catch up to you," Madison informed her father. "I want to have a few words with Gil Rideau first." She refused to call him Jesse, so Jesse anticipated fireworks were about to happen.

Madison smiled at Caroline, "Would you mind if I have a moment alone with...him."

Andy instantly understood the situation, and whisked Caroline back into the house, telling her to wrap up some pieces of pie for Madison and Timothy.

Madison dismounted Timber, and approached Jesse with an icy set to her lips. "Just in case you might have misunderstood," Madison voiced angrily. "I kissed Jesse Kaleb, son of Caroline and Andy. I did not kiss Gil Rideau, nephew of murderer, Harry Rideau."

Jesse's eyes narrowed in retaliation. "Don't you go blaming me for Harry's craziness...and I didn't kiss you...Had no intentions of it."

"And you had no business lying to me. You are an impersonator who..."

"... saved you from getting eaten by a bear, let you keep Timber...and even let you sleep in my bed," Jesse added in self-defense.

Caroline hurried out of the house, anxious to catch Madison before she left to catch up to the other riders.

"Some pie for you and Timothy," she offered, her cheeks aglow from rushing the chore.

Madison took the wrapped pie gratefully and put it in her saddlebag. She threw Jesse an evil eye, and turned to mount Timber. Out of respect, she would not argue with Jesse in front of Caroline or Andy. She glanced down at Jesse from upon Timber. "So what do I call you now?"

"Jesse Randall Kaleb", Caroline cut in proudly, enjoying the sound of the name rolling off her tongue.

Madison looked puzzled.

Jesse laughed at her confusion. "Your Pa will chew off my good leg if you don't get going and catch up to their group."

Madison sighed. She had no more time to find out details. She left quickly, knowing her father would be waiting anxiously down the mountain trail, wondering why she had not caught up to them by now.

"Why didn't you tell her the whole truth?" Andy asked.

"Aaah! Let her wonder what's going on a bit. Her curiosity will have her back on our doorstep before Ma can untie her apron."

13

Madison hurried Timber along, knowing she had stayed longer than she planned and that her father would likely be waiting impatiently down the trail.

Suddenly Timber slowed from a brisk walk to a stop, and stepped back several paces, tossing his head up and down in a nervous manner. Madison trusted the horse's instincts, and did not push him to continue. "What's the matter, fella? Something you don't like up ahead?"

Timber backed up farther and that's when Madison caught sight of the cougar crouched on a large tree branch at the bend in the trail. She backed Timber away slowly step by step until they were a good distance away, never taking her eyes off the cougar. The cat watched her but did not move a muscle from where he waited. Madison did not want to initiate an attack by moving away too quickly. When enough distance was between them, she turned around and rode in the opposite direction, praying the cougar would not follow them, and attack from a different position.

She was not sure how far to circle around to get to the riders on the other side of the cougar. The higher mountain range where the Kalebs lived was not familiar to her. She dared not return to where the cougar was, so decided to detour. She gave Timber's neck a pat. "Guess as long as we aim downward, we should be going in the right direction. Then we can cut back across to the trail."

The terrain was rough and Madison had to travel in a variety of directions to get around boulders and trees and gullies, none of which were familiar to her. After awhile, she did not know east from west or north from south, and certainly had no idea where to cut back to the original path.

She finally pulled Timber to a stop. "I'm lost, boy. Pure lost. I should have just gone back to the Kalebs when I saw the cat. It's getting dark, and Dad will be frantic...and I'm frantic. Where's that cougar now? You'd warn me if he was close, wouldn't you, Timber."

Somewhere high in the mountains, a lonely wolf howled and his call chilled Madison to the bone. She gripped the reins closer. It was dusk, and soon she would not see well enough to travel. She sought a place protected on two sides with a high cliff face to put her back against. Then she gathered a night's supply of firewood quickly before dark, and stood Timber against the high wall beside her. She searched her saddlebag for matches and lit the blaze. Hopefully, the fire would keep unwanted wildlife away.

She retrieved Timber's saddle and sat it upright so she could lean comfortably against it. After a time, Madison remembered Caroline's pie, and opened her saddlebag to remove the package of pie slices. She was ever so grateful that Caroline had given her food, and smiled to think Timothy may never forgive her for eating his portion of the strawberry rhubarb pie. She pulled her blanket closely around her shoulders and stared into the darkness. She would not sleep this night.

ଔଓ

When Madison failed to join the waiting riders, Mel Graham grew impatient. "Caroline is likely stuffing my daughter with pie. I'll go back and hurry her up." He turned to the Sheriff. "You and Tim go on ahead, and I'll be along if Caroline doesn't talk us into staying the night. Don't wait for us. Best you two get going before nightfall." Mel turned back on the trail while Sheriff Bailey and Timothy hurried on down the mountain, aiming to reach the flats before dusk set in.

Mel was gravely frightened to find Madison not at the Kalebs, nor on the trail between him and the homestead. It took only seconds for Jesse and Andy to saddle up and gather some lanterns.

"Too much rock and scrub to find out where she might have left the trail," Andy sighed. "Don't know if she cut out to the east or west of the trail."

"You and Mel take the east. I'll head west," Jesse suggested. "He doesn't know the mountain up here as well as we do, so you two go together. I'll take the dogs. Shoot three times if you find her. I'm surprised Madison hasn't been firing."

"Didn't bring her gun today," Mel informed Jesse with a sarcastic glare. "Too afraid she'd shoot you with it."

Jesse swallowed uncomfortably and didn't reply. He told them to go on ahead, and he turned back to the barn to retrieve a canvas tarp. His keen ears picked up a faint rumble of thunder, and he hurried to roll up the tarp with a bundle of dry kindling inside. He tied it onto the back of his saddle and quickly turned Redtip off the trail to the west. It was not a good thing to be alone in the mountains without a gun, and all three men knew that. Fear gripped his chest as he rode westward, calling her name in hopes that she might soon answer.

Nightfall set in and Jesse lit his lantern to see where he was travelling. It was difficult to know where to look for Madison, as the mountain concealed a thousand gullies and cliffs, and at this time of night, all was wrapped in a dark, forested shroud of pine. He could barely see a couple horse lengths in front of him, even with the lantern glow.

One of the hounds appeared to pick up a scent and he followed the dog, hoping it was following Madison's trail, not some rabbit or fox.

In the distance, Jesse heard the thunder louder than before, and knew a storm was approaching. It was not uncommon in the mountains for storms to come quickly. On one hand, he wanted rain, for it would drive wildlife to seek cover, and not be so interested in Madison as prey. But on the other hand, the cold mountain rain would wash away any scent for the dogs, and not allow for the safety and warmth of a fire for Madison. Even Timber could lose footing on slippery, wet bedrock. He shook his head. He must think positive, and watch that he, himself, did not drop thousands of feet off a cliff in the dim lantern light. He would be of no use to Madison then.

ↂ

Madison heard thunder rolling closer, and the wind began to roar through the top of the pines as the storm front approached. She wished she had chosen a place with better protection overhead from rain. She had been so fearful of predators that she had concentrated on a protected spot where she could light a fire, and had not predicted a storm. At least, she had a waterproof slicker rolled up on the back of the saddle, so she wrapped it around her shoulders, and sat once again in front of her fire. She knew the rain would soon put her fire out, but there was nothing she could do to prevent it. It was too late and too dark to seek a more protected spot. She tried to convince herself that it was safer out here anyway, because wildlife would seek the caves out of the rain, and she didn't relish the thought of sharing a cave with a bear or cougar. The thought brought little comfort when the rain started pelting down in relentless, icy waves. With the fire out, she walked over to Timber and crawled beneath his belly. His barrel was a roof of sorts, and she could trust his calmness not to step on her. She shivered in the cold and pulled the slicker closer.

About three o'clock in the morning, she had her head bowed, letting the rain drip off her slicker hood, when a voice asked, "Any room under there for two?"

She looked up into the welcome face of Jesse, revealed only by flashes of lightning overhead. His slicker glistened in the lightning flashes, and rain ran off the brim of his hat in riverlets. She was so relieved to see him and crawled out from under Timber to throw her arms around his neck, knocking his hat off. He held her close and felt her cold, wet face tremble against his cheek. "It's alright," he comforted. "You're safe now."

"I saw the puma on the trail, and I tried to take a detour and got lost. It got dark so fast," Madison explained with a voice that shook from being cold and damp for hours.

Jesse turned to pull Redtip in closer beside Timber. Thunder boomed and Redtip flinched, but Timber just tossed his head slightly and shook the rain from his mane. Jesse untied a canvas roll from the back of his saddle and walked over to a fallen log nearby, throwing the canvas over the log to form a peeked roof. They both crawled beneath the canvas, and huddled on the soaked ground. "Your slicker is fairly waterproof, so take it off and we'll use it to sit on," he instructed Madison. "I'll take mine off and we can use it to put around both of us. It's the best we can do. I'll start a fire with some dry kindling that I brought."

The two coonhounds stood outside in the drenching rain, staring into the dried tent with mournful expressions. Madison looked compassionately at Jesse and he sighed. "Okay, Toast and Tidbit, get in here, seeing as you helped find her...but if you shake one hair, you're outta here."

The two dogs dashed into the tent space as a clap of thunder boomed overhead. They instantly shook themselves of excess water, and Madison screamed as she was showered with their cold wet spray. Jesse just shook his head as the dogs settled down to share their small dry space. "You two are the worst excuse for guardians that I've ever seen."

Jesse lit the kindling near the entrance. "It's thundering too loud to fire shots right now, but as soon as the storm quietens down, I'll fire three shots to let them know I've found you."

Madison leaned in closer to the fire and felt the heat warm her neck and damp chest.

Jesse leaned forward also and reached out a hand to pull back a fall of her hair, which he feared too close to the flame. "Be careful," he warned.

She turned her face towards him, feeling the touch of his hand holding her hair back behind her ears. He slowly retrieved his hand, letting his fingers slide down across her cheek in a gentle caress. Then he quickly rose to attend the fire.

"Who are you really?" Madison asked, studying his handsome face in the firelight.

Jesse heaved a deep sigh. “It’s a long story. For now, I'll just explain that I am Caroline's first-born, before she met Andy. Her grandfather told her the baby died and put me in an orphanage. I ran away from the orphanage when I was about ten, and was picked up by Guilbert Rideau, Harry's brother, and brought to Riverflats. When Guilbert died, I was sent back east to their sister, and when she died, I stayed with another good man, Sol Barns. When he was killed, I accidently wound up at the Kaleb farmstead on route back to visit Guilbert Rideau's grave. My horse went down in a storm and I had concussion and loss of memory for a while. Caroline believed me to be the son she lost in the river, so we let her be."

"Caroline told me about having a son in Boston before she met Andy," Madison revealed. "So does Caroline think you are her first-born or her second child? I worry for her."

"She accepts the truth now. She got talking about her grandfather, Sterling Lewis, and it was a Sterling who dropped me off at the orphanage as a newborn on the same date her baby supposedly died, so we put the story together, and here I am. That's gotta be some kind of a miracle or twist of fate."

"Not fate," Madison smiled gently. "God's grace."

He smiled in return. "Yes, and by His grace, I'll get you home safely before your father kills me."

Madison laughed and held the slicker open for him to come back and sit beside her to share the raincoat. He pulled the slicker around their bodies, and even though the thunder echoed across the mountain chain and rain poured off the canvas cover like a waterfall, he thought it was one of those times when he really didn't care how wet his socks were, so long as he could watch firelights dance in her hair as she rested her head upon his shoulder.

∞

The young couple eventually drifted off to sleep and Jesse failed to fire the three signal shots to tell Mel and Andy that he had found Madison. When Andy and Mel discovered their small campsite, Mel Graham was in a foul mood at not having been notified. He yelled into the canvas tarp and both Jesse and Madison and the dogs leapt to their feet like a bunch of foxes caught in the hen house.

"You plan on letting us cross the mountains all the way to the ocean before notifying us?" her father snarled at Jesse, as he wrapped a loving arm around his daughter. "Man, you scared us, little girl."

Madison hurried to explain. "You would never have heard the shots during the storm. Then we fell asleep." She gave her father a hug and changed the subject. "The puma was on the trail so I tried to detour around and got lost," Madison explained, "and then night came and the storm. Thank goodness, Jesse and the dogs found me, and he brought shelter and dried wood, or we'd be two drowned rats by now."

Andy patted Madison on the shoulder. "Glad you're safe, child. We was worried some."

Jesse remained silent, half expecting some sort of a thank you from Mel Graham for having rescued his daughter, but not a word of appreciation crossed Mel's lips. So Jesse turned to the canvas tarp and began rolling it up. Andy went over to him. "I'll do that. You ride on home and get dry clothes on, and some of your mother's hot apple cider in you."

"No more mountain riding for you, young lady," Mel Graham declared strongly, and Jesse turned his head around to look at Mel and Madison. He knew exactly what her father was implying, and it had nothing to do with her encountering the puma.

Andy whispered quietly to Jesse. "You gotta prove your worth to the man first, son. Right now, he don't know you from a toadstool." Jesse didn't reply and turned back to pick up his saddle.

Madison led Timber over to where Jesse was now saddling Redtip. He glanced at her, but did not speak.

"Thank you for last night," she said softly. "I hope you don't get pneumonia for trying to keep me warm."

"Likely die of lead poisoning before I die of pneumonia," he said as he proceeded to tighten the cinch on his saddle with short, angry jerks. He didn't like her father treating him like he wasn't a man to be trusted.

Mel Graham yelled across to them, "Time to go, Maddy. Folks will be crazy with worry back home."

Madison waved at her father to let him know she was coming. Then she turned quickly back to Jesse again. "Do phantoms ever go fishing at Runaway River?"

Jesse looked at her and then across at her father. A man can feel when a woman is his match and so he reached out and put a hand on Timber's chest and slowly backed up the big bay just enough so that Mel could not see the young couple behind the horse. Jesse curled one hand around her curly locks and pulled her face towards his. Gently, he let his lips touch hers and linger there for a moment, giving her a small taste of what the future might bring. Then he swung up into the saddle on Redtip. The hooves of his flighty chestnut danced with eagerness to get going, stirring up the fog around the horse's hooves. He smiled at her, and turned Redtip into the mountain mist.

Madison's heart soared high above the timberline. She had a feeling the fishing would be good at Runaway River.

Also available from Verna Elliott Hutlet

www.ingramcontent.com/pod-product-compliance
Lightning Source LLC
Chambersburg PA
CBHW030232180626
46810CB00008B/3088

* 9 7 8 0 9 9 1 7 8 6 8 5 5 *